don’t fear the reaper

sara dennison

Summary

A young woman is put to the test when her dead sister returns as what she used to hunt and asks for her help when her friends are getting killed off. Will she be able to handle reconnecting with her little sister while being surrounded by the very creatures she was trained to kill from a young age? Tackling the strange task by making new friends and with old enemies surfacing to play, will she be able to catch a murderer before it's too late? Reapers, hunters, magic, Death, who will be the last wo(man) standing?

There have been many people who helped with the process and production of this novel, many people who inspired me to follow my dream and I thank each and every one of you.

Table of Contents

1 KNOCKING ON DEVIL'S DOOR

It felt dingy, like a million others I'd been to in the last couple of weeks. They all start to look the same after a while. At least it seemed clean enough. I simply sat at the bar. My drink had been gathering heat in front of me. I came to get drunk but once I had gotten here, I just wasn't feeling it anymore. Whatever *it* was.

My thoughts had gotten the better of me. Again. This has been the eighth bar I've been to in the last week, and it's only Thursday. Just another dump to soothe my soul. I didn't even bother to move when the figure from across the room sashayed over. I noticed her over there, she was hard to miss.

She wore a mini skirt, a black leather number. Who chose to wear that on a weekday, I only had one idea but I couldn't say it bothered me. I watched her the entire way, whether she noticed it or not, I couldn't say. Her skirt moved up as she strutted over, I wondered if she knew how distracting it was. My eyes followed every inch of skin being revealed. But that is exactly what I wanted her to be. Distracting.

"Looks like you could use another drink, little darlin'." She decided to ignore the fact that there was one sitting in front of me, untouched. That's the thing about these women, they only see what they want to see. Looks like she wanted to see me. And wanted me to see a whole lot of her, leaning forward far enough for me to get a good look down her low-cut blouse.

I turned to get a good look at her, might as well if she was insisting. My eyes followed the trim of her thin shirt, it looked like she might've cut it herself to expose more skin. I looked back at the drink in my hand.

"Yeah, I'm nursin' this one, hon." I didn't necessarily want her to go away but I wouldn't have minded if she chose to take a hike. I guess I didn't sound off-handish enough.

Without looking up from my glass, I watched her from my peripherals. She signaled to the bartender, who invested herself in flirting with two men as far from the door as they could get. "Two scotches, please."

She'd been down there ever since she got the drink wasting space in front of me. Maybe her rent was due. I might have been being harsh but so far she isn't proving me wrong. Not like she knew my internal dialogue on her life choices, anyway. Besides, who am I to judge?

The bartender seemed irritated, probably didn't want to interrupt her evening planning for after work, or maybe during if we left early enough. But she plopped the drinks down just the same. Not that this one would have ever noticed but I watched her as she headed away from us, checking on the one other patron sitting at the bar.

"Thanks, Jo." The bartender grunted and went back to the gentlemen, right back at it as if nothing had distracted her. Yupp, they were all the same. Just looking for the next score, the next dime, the next hot night. Just like me.

"Try this one, sweet thang." She held both glasses. I turned my whole body to face her head-on. I grabbed one of them, our fingers grazing. She didn't give it to me at first, lingering her hand on mine, a silent tug-of-war. I raised an eyebrow.

I didn't play into her game, though. I had my own to play. Once she released it, I downed it in one big gulp, save for the little dribble that ran down my chin. I quickly wiped it away. I enjoyed the burning sensation that lingered in my throat. Had a feeling I'd need to be drinking like a fish for this one.

"Wow, I like a woman who can drink," a quick glance at her from under my lashes, "So what's your story? What's a pretty girl like you doin' all alone?"

Of course, I got a talker. "My father just died. So, I'm drownin' my sorrows." I said it too bluntly. Cursing at myself internally, I looked down at my drink, trying to cover it up with reticence. Everything leads to a game when you look at it in the right lighting. And I am a hell of a player.

"Oh, no, I'm so sorry," she said it like she has known my pops for years. She ran her hand up my thigh, trying to be comforting, I guess. I've run this enough, that's how they all act. Until it's time for the end game to be revealed. Ever so caring, like they actually wanted to listen, not just get you back to some sort of bed and into your wallet. But it's just that, an act.

Once I started talking, I couldn't seem to stop myself. Or at least that's how I wanted it to seem. She's the one who wanted to listen so much.

Tears welled up in my eyes, "Yeah, and my mom's been gone for a couple years now and I'm the only kid so now I'm all alone." I tried to say it with a choke, as if I was really crying. I even spilled my old beer a little bit, like my hands were shaky from emotion. I could've rolled my eyes at how easy this had become.

"You, poor baby. I'm Morgan."

"Rhydian."

"You shouldn't be alone right now, why don't you co…." She got cut off before she could even tell me her price.

"You know, it's funny because I happen to know your mother is very much alive and kicking. And you have two sisters and a brother. Shame on you."

I froze. That voice was all too familiar. I sobered immediately, which I shouldn't have with Morgan right in front of me, studying my face. She scuffed and got up. Before she found herself another victim, she slapped me.

"Pig!" It stung but I couldn't help but watch as she left.

"Mm. Real shame. She seemed so nice." The voice came again.

"You can't be here." I put my head in my hands and rubbed my eyes. No, this can't be. It just can't.

“This isn’t possible.” I fluttered my hand across my arm, where there lay a scar that came from a long-lost memory with that voice. I wanted to get up and run but something kept me rooted to my bar stool. Maybe it was pain, maybe regret, but deep down I knew what it was. I knew it was the guilt. I had, after all, let her die.

“Oh, it’s very possible, little darlin’.” She mocked Morgan’s voice.

“I watched you die.” Real tears welled up this time, “Allison, I felt the life leaving your body.” I turned to look at her. And by god, she was still just as beautiful as ever. Stunning, just standing there in the poor lighting. This was no place for her. I wanted to get her out of here, my instinct to protect stronger than ever. But at the same time, I didn’t want to go anywhere with her. Anywhere near her.

“It’s possible. You know it is.”

“How?”

“You know that, too.”

I closed my eyes and let the tears roll down my face. I let the heat center me. After a second, I brushed them away. I tried to think of any excuse for how she could be standing here except for the obvious one, the one I prayed to not be true.

My face became hard, “You’re a reaper.”

I’ve been in the biz long enough to know they didn’t make just anybody something else. You had to be a real baddie, or just special. I didn’t want to think of which category she fell into. I didn’t even want to know that she was other.

Allison smiled and let her horns come out, they glittered in the bar’s light, completely ignoring the fact that we were not alone. The ease in which they just materialized out of nowhere, it was uncanny. They were red at the tips but faded to black the closer they got to her head. Fitting. She even did it like it was nothing. As if she didn't remember what I did for a living. Or used to. Like she didn’t remember who we were. What we both have done.

My face crumbled as I looked at them. So out of place on her angelic face. I held my breath for a moment. When I let it out again, I felt empty. Whatever came next, I wouldn;t fight it.

“Are you here to take me? I haven’t died yet.” I wouldn’t have minded, in all honesty. To get out of this god forsaken world would be a blessing. And I could spend the rest of my afterlife with her. Yeah, I wouldn't mind that at all.

Allison laughed, the sound of angels singing and birds chirping. At least to me, it was. The same laugh that I had heard all my life. I closed my eyes. Pain returning with the memory of how I lost her, of what I had done.

"No. I'm here because I need your help, Rhyder." No one has called me by that name since, well... Since the world went to shit.

"Why me? I've been out of commission for a long time now." She didn't forget, after all. She might've been different, not stupid. No matter the face or the laugh. She wasn't the same. I told myself I wouldn't go with her. I cannot help her kind. I kill them.

She stepped closer to me, reaching a hand out to me. I flinched away from her and she hesitated. Then she continued putting her hand on each side of my face. They were freezing. I guess I shouldn't have been surprised, she was dead after all. I had no choice but to look at her face. I wanted to memorize her face all over again. I wanted to believe that she was here and real and still the same. My old Allison. But those hands kept me from believing. I knew what she was. I knew we'd never be the same. She wasn't even a *she* anymore, she was an it.

"You are still Rhydian Gregerson. You track and hunt and kill and win. You are still my best friend. And now I am asking you for help. Please. Rhyder, there's no one else I can go to."

"Surely there are other hunters who would help you. Everyone has a price." I tried to argue but it was useless.

"But none of them are you. You are the best of the best and you know it. And so do I and so do they. You are right, everyone does have a price. What is yours, I wonder?"

I looked into those eyes. I could go with her. I could pretend for a little while. Closing my eyes again, I thought about what had happened to her again. I could help her.

I kept my eyes closed. "You were always my weakness, little sister."

Allison hugged me. "Thank you."

I hugged her back. Other than the change in temperature, she felt the same. Yeah, I could pretend for a little while. And when she tried to pull away, I squeezed harder. I felt her soften against me. She thought just like my baby sister. She kept standing there until I released her, she didn't try to pull away any sooner. Giving me all the time I needed.

"I'm real. This is all real. But we must go. Now. Come on."

I let go of her like she was on fire. I nodded my head quickly. "Right, uh, fill me in on the way. I'll drive."

"I know a faster way." She grabbed my arm and dragged me towards the door.

We started running and I tried to protest but before I knew it, we were running directly for the door, I thought for sure she was trying to knock me out or that I was crazy and hallucinating all of this. But we didn't stop until we were about to run into it. Or so I thought.

We went through it, but the other side was not night nor a dingy parking lot. We were in a forest, in the middle of the day. I guess I had just forgotten the talents that reapers possess. It's been a while.

"What'd you say?" My ears were ringing. My vision was blurry. I tried to catch my bearings, holding my arms as feelers, making sure I didn't stumble and fall.

She extended her arm towards me and I flinched back, Allison simply slapped my hands away. She pressed two fingers to my temple and it stopped, I inhaled sharply. I blinked at her. My sight coming into focus.

"I said it was a short trip."

I put my hands on my knees and worked on my breathing. "Yeah, I woulda settled for my bike, there, sis."

"I like things fast," she giggled. That used to be an old joke between us. I tried to laugh.

"My bike is fast." I argued.

"I'm faster."

"Yeah, always gotta one up me," I stood up to my full height, "Well, almost always." This time I did laugh. She rolled her eyes. It felt like old times. Well, almost. The smile fell from my face.

"Come on. It's this way."

"What is?"

"Home."

I accepted the confusion. Allison never liked to tell me anything, not in a straightforward way at least.

We trekked through the woods for a little while in silence. The woods were very sparse, I couldn't even get a good pinpoint on where we were and took a deep breath, trying to see if I could smell anything that could give me a clue. I smelled something else instead.

"Fire." I inhaled again to catch a whiff of what was burning. It was simply wood, it seemed, maybe some foliage. I cursed that witch for giving me enhanced senses but by god, do they come in handy.

She stopped to look at me. "Where?"

I cocked my head and sucked in some air again. I could hear the crackling of flames. "'Bout forty clicks that way." I pointed off towards my right. All she did was smile.

"What?"

She kept walking. I started after her.

"What?"

I never did get my answer. The trees were very sparse, indeed. They seemed to move without a breeze, though. There was a crack from above in one of the trees. I shoved Allison against a tree. My body shielding hers. I pulled a knife from one of my boots and threw before I even saw anything. There's no point in having good senses if you don't pay attention to them, I cursed at myself.

"What the hell?" Allison sputtered once I got my weight off of her.

I moved out of her line of sight. "Friend of yours?" I was smug, I may not have been paying attention to what my senses were trying to tell me but I still didn't miss.

There was a man. Well, ish. On the ground, my knife was embedded in his shoulder. I frowned, smugness fading, that's not where I was aiming. And now he was growling at me.

"Come on, big boy. Want to play?" I had no second thoughts about baiting a pissed off reaper. Call me crazy. Or maybe I just had a death wish. Maybe both.

"Clark!" Allison called out to him. I looked at her and she pushed past me to go to him.

"Clark? Who the fuck is Clark?"

"It's complicated!" She yelled again as she knelt on the ground next to him.

"Goddamn it." I muttered. Walking over, I glanced up in the other trees. My breath hitched.

"We have company. Allison, it's time to get the hell out of here." Every tree seemed to be filled with them. I really need to pay more attention. Or maybe they were just able to hide from me.

I was still looking up, Allison never responded. "Allison, zap us out of here."

She was distracted with her little boy-toy. So still no response, "Allison!"

"They're friendlies, Rhydian!"

"Hey, you brought me here to do what I do best. I'm doin' it." I already had multiple knives in each hand. I was ready if even one of them made a move I didn't like. I couldn't kill them all but I'd be damned sure I tried and took as many of them with me as possible.

I bounced on my toes, waiting. I had a couple more knives stowed away in my boots. Just have to make it work. I considered throwing them to Allison but I still wasn't too sure who's side she would be on.

"Rhydian, stop!" Allison turned to look at me. Her eyes were white. Everywhere. That's what happens when you piss off a reaper. I swore under my breath.

"Whoa." I tried to say it in a soothing tone but I was hungry for a fight. It showed in my voice. I crouched so she was taller than me. Reapers have nasty tempers. And she was already moving her head, watching my every move, in the most uncanny way.

"Easy there. Easy, sis." If she needs to be the biggest dog, I won't bite. But my patience was running thin. And then she snarled at me.

"Hey! Control yourself. You are not an animal." I snapped back. Well, no one could say I didn't try to take the higher road.

She didn't seem to hear me. Allison put a hand on Clark's side, leaning over him but towards me. Just like she was an animal. More protective of him than me, I would try not to take offense to that.

"I said stand down!" I never used the power of reason to back someone into a corner. I liked knives better. And I had only one of those things on me that I would use on her.

I could feel the eyes of the lot of them, staring down at us. They haven't moved which somewhat surprised me. I already hurt one of their friends and based on how this encounter is looking I might injure another one. Of course I would never hurt my sister, but they don't know that. Of course there is the chance that they just don't give a damn.

"Come on, sis. You called me here. I assume it wasn't to kill me." All the other reapers released their holds on the trees, they rained down around us. Okay, looks like they do care.

"You need to be the biggest bad? Fine but I'm not apologizing." I dropped all my knives, making sure none were too far away if I needed to make a quick grab for one. I raised my hands. Mostly for dramatic effect, since I was not surrendering to shit.

"Al, I'm okay. Just surprised me, is all." The reaper on the ground spoke for the first time. Everything else went quiet and we all looked at him.

His voice did something for her that mine could not. She looked back at him and cocked her head, which I sadly had to say was unnatural, almost making me gag. He moved his hand so it rested on her cheek. I watched as she sank into it. I heard Clark laugh. I had to look away from the affection. I tried not to be hurt that she didn't listen to me.

I looked to the ground, ignoring those around me. I didn't think they would do anything now that it was calm. I looked at the leaves and roots as if I was fascinated by them.

I crouched down, slowly picking up each blade, only standing fully when Allison helped Clark up. It was evident that he could not do it alone. She did let go of him when he lurched in my direction. I couldn't quite call it walking.

Before I saw it, I landed on my ass, my face blowing up with pain. It was surprising I didn't pass out. Note to self, don't stab that one. I heard a groan and my knife landed next to me. I looked up at him, debating whether it was a good idea to try and put it back in him. I never read those notes anyway.

"Don't worry, I won't apologize either."

He did give me a hand up, though. I decided to let it go.

I looked at Allison, " I want him on my team. LIke all the time."

She laughed, it sounded forced but I'd accept it for now. I looked around me. This was the first time I got a good look at them.

"Jesus, I've never seen so many reapers in one place." There were more now than there were in the trees but I have no idea where they came from.

Allison walked up beside me. Her eyes were back to normal if not a little bloodshot. She led me through the crowd, they moved out of our way. Out of her way. I looked down at her.

"You the biggest bad, sis?"

Allison smiled, for real this time. She even blushed. "You've missed a lot, sister." We kept on walking, Clark was right behind us. "We have all become warriors."

My eyebrows raised, that didn't make any sense. "Reapers are only supposed to collect the dead. Bring them to the other side. Why would you need to fight? *Who* would you need to fight?"

I was looking at Allison but she isn't the one who answered. "Someone is killing my reapers. Not allowing them to pass over. We were hoping you could answer the second question."

"How would I know who was ki...." I didn't finish my question as I was looking for who spoke. The reapers all fell to their knees, I would've laughed if it didn't seem so serious, except Allison and Clark. And the one in front of me. This one felt different. Colder. I glanced back but kept walking forward. I don't know why but I felt the need to get as close to her as possible.

"And who are you?"

"She's Death," Allison said it from her place behind me. She didn't sound scared.

I laughed. "This? This is Death? Oh, bravo, sister, you had me fooled. Am I dead or crazy?" I laughed again but while I had spun to speak to Allison, Death had come up close behind me. I turned back around and came face to face with her. My smile vanished as she leaned into me.

She placed a finger on my forehead and pressed it against me. Our chests were pressed together and I saw Death blow something toward me, it smelled as if it was cigarette smoke, and then I saw nothing but blackness.

I heard Allison gasp as I sucked in a breath. I could feel her lunge towards me but somebody pulled her back. I reached out for her. I felt nothing. I tried to turn and look for her, something must be wrong. I turned back towards Death. But all I saw was my dad.

"Daddy?"

He was running through the woods. But not the same forest I was just in. I could hear growling. I started running, too, but I don't think I was really moving. I tried to catch up to him, to let him know what was happening. I couldn't help him.

"Dad, what's going on? Why are we running?" But I knew what I was seeing. I stopped trying to move. I knew exactly what this was. I never believed the stories. I never knew Death was real or that she could actually do these things. This was power that came straight from Hell. And she was using it on me.

It doesn't matter that I stopped chasing after him, I could see him, as if I was staring at a screen. But I wasn't. I could smell his sweat, and the trees, and the mud.

"Go, dad run!" I tried to yell to him but he didn't seem to hear me. Of course he couldn't, this wasn't in present time, this was a moment in the past that I had never wanted to see. I put my hands over my mouth to hold back a scream. I knew what this was. I couldn't help him. It had already happened.

"No, dad! Faster!" I could feel heat running down my face. I knew I was crying but I didn't care. I could yell and cry and he wouldn't hear a thing. I was just looking at a ghost of him. No matter how much of a bastard he was in life, he was still my father. And no one deserves what's coming. I didn't want to see this. I knew what happened but seeing was something entirely different.

I watched dad trip and drag himself behind a tree. It wasn't a tree big enough to hide him. Not from a werewolf pack. I remember that night. He wouldn't let me go with him. He was reloading his gun when he became surrounded. His face was still. He had to work to see what was in front of him. Shots rang out and he made a run for the path that he had just made for himself straight ahead.

"No, daddy!" I knew what happened next. I always knew. I just never thought I'd have to watch it. "No." That came as a sob. I choked on it and started to cough. I didn't care.

One jumped out and grabbed a hold of his leg, biting down, dragging him backward into the darkness. I let my scream out right along with his. The other werewolves joined in on the feast. I let myself fall to my knees. Soon enough the night became silent except for the sounds of feeding. I let all my hurt and anger crawl out with the tears that I've held in for far too long.

My hands were fists on the ground. That's what I saw when the vision was gone. My hands clamped around grass. I waited for the tears to stop running before looking up.

Death was waiting in front of me. "I'm sorry. I very much dislike doing that, but you didn't believe me. I had to make you understand. I can make you forget, if you'd like." Death reached a hand out to touch me again.

I quickly slapped it away. "Don't you fucking touch me." I tried to sound brave but I'm sure I looked horrified.

"What did she show you?" Must've been Clark. I glanced up at him, he looked horrified, too. I crinkle my eyebrows because behind it, he looked pleased. I put my head in my lap.

"Dad's death." I whispered. I heard Allison's sharp intake of breath, she must have known based on what I was saying, must've been a shock. I sat there like that for a while. I knew they were all staring at me but to hell with them. They can't judge me. They don't understand.

"What do you want from me?" I got back on my feet. I refused to make eye contact with anyone but I knew they were all still staring. I kept my eyes down. As soon as I was stable something ran by my feet, almost knocking me over again.

"What the fu.." I fell into Clark. He shoved me up straight.

"She has a thing with goats." Clark responded.

Then I saw it. Sure enough, laying at her feet was a goat. "I do not want a thing. Ally, here," she stepped up when her name was spoken, "said you could help. So, help." Death said it as if it was that simple.

I shook my head. "Okay, " how does one say no to Death, my voice sounds scratchy, I cleared my throat, "Okay, first of all, there are plenty of hunters out there that kill you guys all the time, what's so different now?"

Death didn't seem too inclined to answer. Allison did, instead," Reapers come from souls that are stuck on this plain of existence. So when a hunter kills one of us, our souls will just move on how they were originally supposed to but whatever is killing us now..” She stopped. I realized that she was scared. I looked around, they were all scared.

“Whoever is killing my reapers now is wiping them out of existence. No heaven. No hell. Just gone.” Death finished it, looking out at her reapers as if they were her children. I guess in a way they were.

This didn’t seem possible. I never heard of such a thing, which was something I was not about to tell my baby sister and her big bad boss.

I ran my fingers through my hair, trying to think. “Alright, alright,” I walked in a small circle, “What do we know?”

“There have been four murders so far,” a girl spoke up from the group. I wonder if these people knew what I did, who I was. Not that it really mattered at the moment.

I searched for who said it. “Mave, step forward.” Clark ordered. I made a mocking face behind him.

Allison came up behind me. “She was having a fling with Clayton, the first one who died.”

“Who was the next?”

"Belle." That was Death. I glanced back at her, shivering.

"Any relations? Friends?"

"Mason and William, her brothers." That was Clark once again. I was about to ask for only one of them to speak. They were all going to give me a headache.

"Next?" I put a hand to my temple, trying to stop the inevitable.

"Cinder."

I glanced at Allison for the next questions but she just shook her head. Moving on, then.

"And the last?"

"Mykie."

"Relations?"

"None." I think they all said it at once. Talk about creepy. I rubbed my hands over my face, trying to rub away the last remains of the vision before I had to go to work.

I took a deep breath, running my fingers through my hair. It's like I couldn't stop moving. Must have been the white smoke.

"Alright, how did they die? Same M.O., I'm assuming? Where and when? Any suspects or even knowledge of what could do this?" There were too many questions, most circling around Death, and it felt like there wasn't very much time. I couldn't focus with her around me.

"Just breathe," Allison was still by my side. I almost got offended. Mom used to tell me that. Before she left us. I gave her a dirty look anyway. But she knew it helped. I was a big girl; I could do this. After all, is it not my job to catch and kill evil? Even if the evil is killing other evil.

Death stepped up to my other side, I could feel the cold radiating off of her, like it wanted to consume me and I wasn't sure if I'd stop it if it chose to. I sensed that Death was the warmest one here. I couldn't even decide if I truly wanted her away from me or not.

"They had their throats slit and eyes appeared to be burned out, evidence of a struggle. They all put up a fight. All their places have been trashed. It seems to be the same person.The eyes are the windows to the soul, so we're under the impression that they're being burnt out or possibly stolen. Any friends of yours into that?" Clark was kind enough to answer my questions.

I tried to step up to him but Allison held me back. Hunters weren't dogs and we certainly weren't monsters. We were just doing our jobs. His voice was irritating, too. The way he says everything like a cop. I don't like cops much. They just get in my way. I almost hoped he would, too.

"Just because it looked the same doesn't mean it was." Nothing is as it appears to be. Doubtful but still.

Death chuckled, "Yes, but we know something that only the killer would know." It seemed a very inappropriate time to laugh.

"And what's that?"

Allison looked at me, solemn. "He's taking their horns." Hers grew at the thought. I could see the sparkle come off the red tips. I glanced at Clark, his eyes had turned red. A reaction to Allison, I'm sure. I don't even think they noticed how they affected each other. I could only imagine how dangerous that will turn out to be.

Souvenirs. Great. I love the sadistic ones. That's an M.O. alright. "Are you sure nobody else knows?"

"Positive. We glamoured all the scenes and they'd only been dead a couple of hours when we found each of them."

"You can glamour?" I directed that at Allison.

"Rhyder, not the point." she chided me, but that did not hide her blush.

“Sorry, right.” I wasn’t sorry but I tried to be serious. This was such an awkward situation for me. Talking to the dead about the *really* dead. I walked over to the first one who spoke.

“Mave, right?” She nodded.

I put a hand on her upper back and led her away from the others. “Tell me what happened.” The only one who tried to follow was the goat, I paid him no never mind. I doubt he would tell our secrets.

“It was really an all-around boring day. No one had died on my round,” it bothered me how nonchalant she was about that but I didn’t press, “I was supposed to meet Clayton at a local dive bar. The kind where questions aren’t asked.”

“Supernatural bar.” I filled in the blanks, nodding. I’ve been to a few. For business, of course.

“Right and he was late. Which he never is. So naturally, I was concerned.”

“Naturally.“ I muttered.

She ignored me. “ I went to his place to see what was wrong. Maybe he just took a nap or something. “ She paused there. Looking off in the distance like he might suddenly wake up. She started to cry. Now what the hell was I supposed to do with that? I debated patting her shoulder, maybe throw a 'there, there' out but I thought better of it.

"Wait," I had stopped her from walking farther, the goat resting between us,"if reapers pick up human souls, who picks up yours?"

"Death." She said it as if there was no other answer, she still didn't return her eyes to me. Mave walked on, almost in a trance.

"Death, right, of course, silly me." I murmured to myself more than to anyone else. I could taste the sarcasm. Not that there were any souls to pick up in this case. I jogged to catch back up with her.

"Death's the one who found them all. I got there in time to see that Clayton's soul wouldn't be moving on."

"And you don't think that's a bit suspicious?"

"No." Mave said it plain as day. I don't think there's any way I could explain it to her the way I see it. Death is a god to these people. But not to me.

"She just happened to find them all. She didn't even seem too concerned about it. If someone killed my babies, I'd be pissed. Death didn't bat an eye." I stopped there, only because I noticed the goat wasn't there anymore. "Ah, hell," I muttered under my breath," Fucking snitch!" That I yelled.

"You are seriously insinuating that Death killed her own reapers?" Mave seemed upset.

I looked away and then right back at her. "Yes." It wasn't my problem if it upset her, I was here to do a job.

"She has no motive. Why would she do that? Answer me that."

"I'm not here to answer the why. I'm here to answer the who." I honestly didn't know why she would do that. I was ready to leave already. Truth be told, I just didn't know anything. And I didn't like that.

"Unbelievable." She huffed and started back the way we came.

"Hey, I'm not done with you here!" I had to shout for her to hear me.

"Yeah, well, I'm done with you."

"Well, that was rude." I didn't bother to follow her. I walked a little farther away from the camp. I wondered where this forest led to. I still had no idea where I was. Maybe it ended on a cliff. I wondered if I was brave enough to jump.

I sat down against a tree. It felt like hours that I've been walking. It probably was only one. Mave would already be back in the camp. Maybe Allison would ask me to leave.

Realize what a bad idea this was. I thought about what I told Mave.

It's never that simple. It's never the first answer you come upon. I learned that from dad. Bastard had to go and get himself killed. If only he'd let me go with him. If he was alive just a week longer, Allison would still be with me. Really with me. Not dead. Well, mostly dead.

I don't know if I wished she was really dead or not. She seems happy. Here. With Clark. Not with me. Maybe she's better off without me. I couldn't protect her the first time around. Who's to say I can this time? What if this killer comes after her and I'm not there to protect her? Would she be better off dead?

"I won't tell her that is what you think."

I jumped. Reflexes had my hand down my boot for a knife before I realized who was talking. Death was standing next to me. As if sneaking up on people was okay and perfectly normal to her. I don't even know if she appeared or just walked up beside me. I put my head in my hands, there was just way too much that I didn't know here. I was too distracted. That's dangerous. She was dangerous. I had to remember that. Or we were all in deep shit.

"So, what? You can read minds now? You here to kill me, too?" My words had no bite. I was far too tired.

"You know I didn't kill my reapers. And you also know they are my favorite of God's creations and I do not want them in a panic."

I shrugged. "What's it matter what I think? Your people are still being killed. Why can't you stop this?"

Death sighed and sat next to me, our knees grazing, "It's been a long time since I've been a horseman. My powers are not what they once were."

I laughed. "Death has gotten soft."

She looked offended, I thought I might have stepped over the line, then she laughed, as well," No one dares to speak to me like that. It is refreshing."

"I won't tell if you won't." It was a strange sound to hear from a horseman of the apocalypse but it washed over me. Refreshing. Just like she said.

Death giggled again. "Deal." She stood, pulling me up to her side. "Come, there is something I think you would like to see.

2 READY PLAYER ONE

We walked together in silence. It wasn't awkward like I thought it would be. With her forcing my father's death upon me and everything. It was quite comforting, actually. Death wasn't that bad, a bit bossy. Oddly bubbly. She chuckled. I glanced at her under my lashes.

"Sorry." She said and stopped smiling. I wasn't sure exactly why. But then we came to the opening to the camp. I didn't pay attention before. It looked like a grove, a big cave, really. It was beautiful, the roof opened upward, sunlight filtered in everywhere, even though the sun should've been going down by now. There were trees everywhere, thicker than the forest outside. Moss grew on every surface. I looked back at Death, she was completely poised. We re-entered the camp. This was Allison's home. I understood a little bit more now. It truly was magnificent.

I put my hand on the nearest tree. The moss covering it felt like what I imagined a cloud would. Looking all around me, I took in the fresh air and the tranquil sounds of nature.

My eyes shot towards Death but she was strictly looking onward. I followed her gaze.

The reapers were all standing in a large circle, surrounding something. Sounds like chanting came from within. People were moving in the center. A lot of people. The closer we got, I could make out more of the sounds. It was yelling.

Death and I pushed our way through. Well, I pushed. They let Death through. I only followed in her wake. Eventually, we made it to the front.

Clark and Allison were back to back, both holding long knives about the size of my forearm. They were surrounded by seven others. All enclosed by the crowd, making a battle arena.

Allison was wearing yoga pants and a sports bar, all soaked through with sweat, I could see it glistening on her skin. Clark was wearing what looked like basketball shorts and nothing else. He was shining, too. Before it really caught up with me what I was seeing, I thought they had the wrong grips on their weapons, they could easily lose their holdings and lose their knives all together. That line of thought didn't last long.

"What the hell is this?" I accused Death.

I tried to yell to Allison. She looked just as someone lunged for her. I tried to move toward her. Death held me back, her grip like a slab of ice. Allison now had a cut on her stomach, she had fallen. Clark glared at me and picked her up. He had turned them so the one who had cut her was in front of him. He grabbed the reaper by the neck and threw him against the wall of the cave. Rocks came down with him.

They were back to back again. All muscles were tensed, I held my breath. I had a chance to notice that neither were wearing shoes. They moved together. They moved as one. They looked like one. They became one. And I couldn't help but remember when we were like that.

Every lunge, they dodged and retaliated with their own blows. They hit more than they missed. Soon the seven were looking in worse shape than the two were. I just happened to notice that the pair was going easy on them. I knew my sister, different or not. Nobody changes that much. She was holding back. They fought as one. Watching each other's backs and using each other to the best advantages. And every move they made, I tried to make my own to get to her. It was useless but I wasn't going to sit back and watch my sister fight without helping.

I could only watch Clark pick up Allison and she kicked three to the ground. He put her down and they went after two others. Allison got hers down first. She rolled over Clark's back to punch the sixth one out of bounds, slicing down with her knife to make sure she stayed that way. They both threw their knives at the last one. Aiming too high to kill. They were on each other there. Staring down the others, just in case one might want to try again. The pair still moved as one person. Death walked forward and the pair finally relaxed.

"What the hell was that?" I wanted to know. I needed to know. I shoved Death out of my way, she finally let me. I rushed to Allison, checking her arms and patting her head. The cut on her stomach would heal faster than a human's but not that much faster. Not without help.

"Training." Death said it simply.

I looked between Allison and Clark. Landing back on Allison since her head was still between my hands, she couldn't have moved me if she wanted to. "I have never seen you move like that." I was insanely proud of her. And utterly terrified for her.

I looked back at Death and my gaze did not soften, my voice hard, " They could've killed her."

"They could have killed him, too. But your concern for him is lacking. Regardless, neither they nor any of them are dead. Funny how that works."

I glanced down at Allison," Why'd you take on seven?"

Clark laughed, "There was actually eight. One got knocked out pretty quick."

I ignored him. My eyes locked on my baby sister. "Eight?"

"Biggest bad, remember? We have to be prepared for anything."

"That's bullshit. You could've been killed."

"Not with me around." Clark butted in, stepping in front of her, knocking my hands from holding her still. As if he'd have to protect her from me. I stepped up to him. We were nose to nose and if I could've, I would've gotten closer.

"Did I ask you, tough guy? What happens when you're not around? Huh? What happens then? What happens if she's alone when that freak show comes around again? Answer me that. She could've been killed tonight."

Allison stepped out from around Clark. "Rhydian." She hesitated, almost as if she knew her next words would hurt me, "I'm already dead." They did.

"Well, apparently you could be deader!" I choked on my next breath. I crinkle my eyebrows against it. Trying to ignore the pain. "I couldn't protect you then." I took a step back, looking, again, at everything around me. It didn't look very beautiful anymore. "It's my fault you're dead. It's my fault you're here."

"I know." She didn't even try to deny it. She walked over and held me in her arms, I fell to the ground and she fell with me.

"I'll protect you this time." I didn't know if she could even understand me, I was hyperventilating.

"Shh. I know. It's alright." She smoothed my hair down with her hand. Rocking us back and forth as if I were a child.

It had been my mistake that had gotten her killed. I had made the decision to split up and plant the trap. I knew she wasn't ready for a hunt but I thought she'd never be ready until she did it. She was right. My baby sister had died because I wanted her to grow up faster. Just like dad had made me. I couldn't get to her when she started screaming. We hadn't been the only ones that split up. It had worked out better for them. But I killed them all.

"I'm so sorry, Allison. I wasn't fast enough. I am so sorry." I held her tight in my arms. I looked up at Clark, who was staring at me. "You protect her. With your life, do you hear me? If you ever so much as live for one second more than her, I will end you. Am I making myself clear?" I pulled her even closer, if she were alive, she wouldn't have been able to breath. That didn't stop me from trying.

"I will." He didn't even hesitate.

I held on to her as tight as I could. "Rhyder, you gotta let me go."

Night was falling fast. Eventually, I did let her go. The cold had begun to seep into my bones. I would've lived with that forever if I could have my sister back. But she wasn't mine anymore. She was his. She was Death's. She was her own.

I knew Death could hear me think all of this. That's why I wasn't surprised when she pulled me up by the elbow. "It is getting late. I will take her to a safe place." I don't think Allson understood why I needed a safe place but I knew what Death meant. Nowhere where I could jump off a cliff or wallow in self pity. I wasn't going to be alone tonight. I didn't know if I should curse god or thank the devil for that.

Death continued. “It is prime time, everybody. Stay in pairs and get to work. Fly, my pretties.” She seemed to be done, based on the fact that she was now dragging me through the quickly dispersing crowd, toward very large trees. I looked up.

“Oh my god,” was all I could manage to say. There were tree houses up there. Like actual houses, “I thought reapers don’t sleep.”

“They do not need to, some like to, though. Either way they need to stay somewhere and since nobody seems to be safe, I brought them to my haven.”

“All of these are yours?”

“Yes. And I do not usually have guests.” I didn’t ask any more questions, just followed her.

She led me to a rope ladder. I climbed it. She floated up next to me as I did. It was kind of weird but I was getting used to weird, even if I’ve only known her for a couple of hours. Death grows on you. The top was just as extravagant as it looked from below. I guess I’d think anything in a tree was great. I’ve never actually seen a tree house. But this was house upon house connected with rope bridges. It seemed to be forming a giant circle. The fighting pit was in the dead center. I probably shouldn't say dead. It was fantastic anyway.

"Will I be staying with Allison?" I wondered.

"No, your sister and Clark share a cabin."

Ugh, gross. "What's going on with them?" I looked down as we walked. I wasn't sure if I wanted to know the answer. I pretended that I was watching my step. I don't know why, she could hear everything I was thinking. Pride, I guess. Maybe dignity. It didn't seem that I had much of either of those after my very short time here.

"According to my intel, they are best friends. That is all, I believe."

That made me laugh, I could see what they were, I guess I just wanted a second opinion. "You're intel isn't worth shit then." I continued to follow her. I didn't bother asking who her intel was. And she didn't seem to feel the need to share. I assumed it was the same way she knew to come talk to me in the forest. That damn goat. It also didn't matter because it was the worst line of bullshit I've ever heard. There's no way I would believe that for a damn second.

We stopped at the largest house. It was in the middle of all the other buildings. Death's cabin, I was assuming.

"That is correct." The door was beaded strands, she held them aside for me. I didn't expect that from her. Even with her bubbly persona, I was thinking of a black door. Maybe red.

"Why am I staying with you?" I stood at the entrance, not daring to move farther in just yet.

"You are hurting yourself with your own thoughts and if you die, I would prefer for your sister not to be the one to find you. She is our strongest warrior. We need her at full strength. No distractions."

"And here I thought it was because you thought I was pretty." I didn't bother to ask why I was here at all then. And she didn't answer.

"That, too." Death continued as if she hadn't just flirted with me. I sputtered for a moment. Shocked, to say the least. I could tell she was smirking, even if her back was to me.

I followed her further in. "You can sleep here." There was a circular bed in the middle of the room. Several pillows were strewn about, not in any particular design. I could see a throw blanket burrowed under some of them. It looked soft. Nothing else was in it. There was a window that looked out at a lake. So, there was a cliff somewhere around here. If I closed my eyes hard enough and took in a big enough breath, I bet I could smell that water. I didn't bother to try.

"I thought you Death didn't sleep either." I ran a hand around the bed until I faced her, with the bed between us. I wasn't quite sure if I was flirting back or not. But I kind of liked where my thoughts were going.

"Beds are used for more than sleeping." She lingered on those words for a moment, all the sexual tension rising, "Goodnight." I didn't have time to think about it further. She walked to the door in a flutter, the loose dress she wore dancing behind her. She truly was a goddess.

And she left me there. I don't know where she went. I doubted she would have told me if I had asked. I was shocked at her sudden departure but I'm pretty sure she did it on purpose. I smiled and climbed into the bed. I wondered how many others have been brought into this bed. But it felt innocent. Clean and untouched.

I could've sworn I heard someone giggle as I fluffed one of the pillows under my head. I didn't see her for the moment so I didn't know who it was but I had an idea. Maybe I was going crazy. That seemed as logical as anything else that was going on in my life right now. I also could've sworn that this was the most comfortable bed I had ever slept on. Who knew what was going on in my head anymore?

I fell into dreams quickly enough. It has been so long since I've actually been able to sleep. Or actually found myself in a bed. Most nights, or days depending, I just lie awake, thinking. Thinking about what all has gone wrong and how I could make it right or what I could've done to prevent all of this from happening. All the things that have happened to me. To dad. To Allison. How it was all my fault. The usual tools in self torture.

I didn't know at the time that Death had come in to watch over me. She didn't wake me up so I didn't really mind. Not that I could've said anything while being asleep. Besides, she still could've been in my head. And I knew something was there when my dreams stretched into nightmares. It always happened. I had gotten used to riding them out. But someone else was there to fight off my demons. Something standing in the shadows and fighting off the monsters for me. Drawing them away, it was something beautiful. It had a funny shape. Like the shape of a goat, chasing away my worries.

3 COME ONE, COME ALL

I thought I'd wake up in a start since I was in unfamiliar territory. I didn't even remember where I was, for a second. But it didn't seem to bother me. I just opened my eyes, sunlight was pouring in through the window. I didn't notice before that there wasn't a pane on it. A nice breeze was filtering through.

It didn't even bother me that I slept in my jeans, I've done it many times before. I got up, stretching my arms. I was yawning when I felt eyes on me. Those eyes, I found out, were green. Like emeralds shining through water. They took my breath away. I felt trapped in them. I don't think I could have looked away even if I wanted to. She never wore makeup, I noticed. But show me someone with balls big enough to tell her she needed to. Not that she needed to anyway.

"Why, thank you. How flattering." Death was sitting in the empty window sill.

I groaned as I flopped back down on the bed, my face in the covers. "I forgot, so bite me."

Death laughed, it was a very light sound. "I know."

I peeked out at her. "You are a collection of paradoxes."

"It is very strange. I cannot read you as well as you think I do. It is very much hit or miss with you. Very strange, indeed." She sounded like she didn't like the sound of me being very strange but I had always been different. Guess I have the witch to thank for that.

"What witch?" Death was looking out at the other cabins.

"I was on a hunt with my dad when I was four…"

"That is awfully young."

"That's the life of a hunter for you. I was old enough to hand him stuff and use the bathroom by myself so I was old enough to go with him." I laid my head on one of the pillows. "I was handing ammunition to him from the outside and we didn't know that the witch we were hunting had a daughter, too. She disguised her kid as herself and sent her after my dad. And the witch came for me. She got a great deal of juice in me before dad cut her head off. It was like I was high until he finished the job and carved out her heart. Then everything just went into overdrive."

I could see myself back there, I was no longer in the cabin, I was back in that Louisiana swamp. I could smell it still. It was the first thing my new senses took in. I don't think I would ever forget it.

"I busted my eardrum just as a car drove by. It was a painful learning process," I shivered at the memory, "That was the most excruciating pain I had ever been in, but hey, at least I got something out of it. Most people don't." I stopped talking there. I never told anyone that story, not even Allison. It wasn't a bad one. Just never came up. She never knew why I was so gifted in a sense. But I know what other hunters would do if they found out. So I never shared.

Death stood up. I watched as she walked over to me, more like glided. I wasn't sure if I would look down if her feet would be on the ground or not. I sat completely still. My neck had to stretch to look up to her. Death put a hand on my chin to keep my head from escaping. She acted like all she wanted to do was look in my eyes. I looked back. But I didn't believe that for a second. Mischief always lingered behind those emerald eyes.

"What else are you hiding in that pretty little head of yours?"

I yanked my head out of her hand. Getting up and away from those eyes. "Nothing good." I hugged my arms to my body, wandering over to the window. Can you call it a window if it is just a hole in the wall? No glass? I stood there and I stared at nothing.

The sound of movement behind me gave me no relief. "You have a tremendous amount of strength to block me out of your head completely." The feel of a hand on my shoulder made me flinch. She removed it after a second. Not unlike my reunion with Allison in the bar. I wasn't even trying to block her out but now that I knew I could, I'd definitely be working on it. Thanks, witchy.

There were steps coming over towards our cabin. It must've been Allison. Maybe Clark. I honed in on the footsteps. Too light to be Clark but still too small to be Allison, too. I looked over at the door with confusion. I inhaled a breath, out of habit. Then I understood. It was the goat.

Death stared at it for the longest time, almost like they were communicating. Hell if I knew, they probably were. I wonder how the goat got up here. I can only imagine it floating up like Death does, I stifled a laugh at the image.

"Got it. Get back to the scene." Death turned back to me, "It is time to go." She didn't bother elaborating. She pulled my arm and dragged me out the door. I was getting real tired of all this dragging these people were doing. Who do they think they are? They are dead, after all. At least I was still breathing.

"Mind telling me what the hell is going on?" I tried to pull my arm out of her grasp but you try struggling with Death.

"Alright, stop!" I managed to yank her to a halt. She turned to me with exasperation.

"There has been another murder. We have to go."

I let her drag me this time. "Was that so freaking hard?" Death didn't bother to answer, I half expected her to.

I hadn't had a chance to visit the other scenes but I imagined that they looked a lot like this one. There was blood everywhere, that was a given. I thought there would be furniture and the like, broken and knocked over from the struggle but there wasn't. Everything seemed perfectly in place. Everyone seemed extremely nervous about it.

I tilted my head and looked around again. "This isn't right."

Everyone looked at me but I kept focused, moving closer to one of the walls. "No, this isn't right at all. Do you see how this blood splatter is on the wall?" I looked back at Allison, just like old times. I knelt down to get closer but immediately stood back up, pointing.

"The body landed there. There might have been some shaking but this blood is in the wrong place for it," I pointed again, this time to the ceiling and then the wall parallel to us, "It should be up there and there. Not here." My finger landed back to the wall next to us.

Nobody said anything. Allison was dumbfounded, her shadow as well. I glimpsed the goat flitting through doorways over the house. I could smell it, too. Death stayed with me as if I was the one in danger. There was another odor I smelled. I breathed in deeply, like a dog trying to catch a scent. I looked around again.

"What does that mean exactly?" Death finally asked, even though she probably already knew my answer. I was now distracted.

"This whole thing is staged." Which didn't make sense. Staging a scene was usually for maximum horror on discovery. But just moving the body from one place to another wouldn't make it any more terrifying especially for someone like Death who finds them.

I knelt to where the body would have been lying. Death already made sure his soul was gone, just like the others, she did it as soon as we got there. The body was out of sight so out of mind. I couldn't help but wonder if Death was glad of that fact for me.

"You never told me he burnt the horns off." I didn't look at any of them. Just kept examining the scene. Burning them off, I imagined just like cattle farmers do with their bulls.

Allison sounded confused, "We told you he was taking them."

I waggled my finger at her. "Yes but not that he was burning them off."

"Is that important? How he took them?" Clark asked, even though I technically arrowed the question towards Death.

"Maybe, maybe not. Could mean he's not strong enough to rip them or wants to hide the fact that he is. Could mean he is squeamish with blood, but taking in his artwork over there, I doubt that is the case, either." I kept looking, I didn't know what I was looking for exactly. But something was off here. Something else, at least.

"How could you tell they were burnt off anyway? The body has already turned to dust." Allison, always with the questions.

I just tapped the side of my nose. I heard her make a little noise of understanding. I looked at the dust that had gathered. Reaper's bodies always turn to dust after a while. Sometimes it takes minutes, others can last hours. Never really knew why. Maybe I'll ask Death when we're through here.

Death was the one who found all the other reapers, except this one. Why? What makes this one different? Who is this one to Death? Or was he just learning?

"Which one do you think?" Death stood very close. It was literally the relationship between two hunters in one of my favorite tv dramas. Yes, I watch a show about the supernatural and yes, I like tv dramas. I only mentioned that internally in case Death was eavesdropping still.

"You gotta stop doing that."

"Make me." It was a whisper, though I was pretty sure everyone in the room had the senses to hear her.

That phrase didn't help any of the loaded sexual tension I knew was lurking under the surface of us both. Maybe not quite those two characters. Regardless, I refused to cave. I looked her in the eye. “Depends. Who is she?”

I knew it was a girl. I could smell perfume all over the house and there was a grocery bag on the counter containing Tampax. Who knew reapers still had their bodily functions? I guess they are only half dead. I told myself I wasn’t jealous. I had no reason to be. This beautiful creature before me was not mine. Could not be mine. I told myself that I didn’t want her in the first place. Death looked sad but very understanding. I was still trying to figure out if she was eavesdropping when she answered my question.

“She was new. A couple of days old.” That was the only explanation Death cared to give.

“So you would’ve been protective of this one. He wanted to take his time with her. So you would know she suffered and you wouldn’t be able to come and get her.” I figured out what I was sniffing for. One, there was no scent of anyone besides who was in the room in this house and that was centralized to the crime scene. Two, Death’s scent was everywhere. That either meant the killer was in this room or he was very very good at covering his tracks.

“Seems reasonable. But that doesn't help us find her killer.” Clark had followed us into the kitchen, where the body had been found.I was selfishly glad she wasn’t there anymore. There was only about a two hour frame to check their bodies, generally. And we missed it. But hey, no clean up to really worry about.

Allison walked in after him. Even with the body gone I wanted to shield her from the destruction and gore. But that wasn’t my job anymore. She didn’t need that from me. I turned away from them and ended up face to face with Death. Again. The memory of the last time was not a good one. I swallowed around a knot in my throat. She just kept staring at me.

“Um,” I was proud, my voice was steady,” Excuse me?”

Death stepped aside immediately, like she didn’t even realize how close she was to me. ‘But, of course.” She even gave a little bow. It seemed oddly familiar. I could not help but to think of her likeness to a cat. I found it very amusing but I refused to let it show. I continued on.

The house was a circular formation, odd no matter where you are, which I still wasn't sure where that was. I walked around into the living room where we were before. "I don't understand. You said they all put up a fight. And yet there is nothing out of place here."

"We think they cleaned up. Maybe a sign of remorse, or something." That was Allison, they were all following behind me. I would have said that was smart except the taking of trophies contradicts that theory. But it was the only theory we had. Besides, they cleaned up the furniture but left all traces of blood and dust.

This is all a message for me. I held very still. If she wanted the others to know, she would've said it outloud. I tried not to react. I didn't know Death could speak to me in this way. To anyone for that matter. I made an effort not to look at her, or anyone else for that matter. I tried it back.

A message for what? I stared at the ground, pretending to look for clues. Come on, scooby gang.

That I do not know.

Then how do you know it's for you?
"Okay," I turned towards the others, pointedly not glancing at Death," We've seen all we can

here. Let's go to the others." I didn't wait for her to respond.

They nodded and did as I asked. They all attended the other scenes with me. It was like they wanted to protect me but if anything I was the one here to protect them. A killer is something I could handle and I wasn't a reaper. I was the safest one here. I still couldn't get the itch that they were trying to hide something from me though.

I was right before. All the scenes were exactly the same. The reaper had been killed in the kitchen, there must have been a struggle but the killer moved everything back into place. He would've had to have been more careful not to break anything. He even cleaned up the blood and body dust from these crime scenes. But why stage the blood if he was going to hide every other aspect of his crime?

I never expected my day to be so grim. If someone would have told me my dead sister would come back and ask me for help in a murder investigation, I probably still would have believed them, but that's besides the point. There was nothing new to learn from the scenes. I couldn't help on this level. Death thinks this freak show is for her. It might be. I don't even know where to start for something like this. What can kill a reaper and damn their souls while wanting to keep their horns?

We were all standing outside house number one. I told them to wait outside while I did my thing inside. Truly I just wanted some alone time. I never thought I'd want that after being alone for so long but I did. They just consumed all the air around me. Chilling. And whatever they were hiding, they couldn't keep me from finding it on my own.

They didn't even realize that they were stealing something from me, either. Clueless. Just like me, on this case. I sighed. I had to go back out to them. And to how they were. Surrounding themselves with a deadly cold. When I returned out to them, I told Allison that I was going to make a call. Of course Death accompanied me as I started off down the street.

It was a street like any other. I guess not all the reapers wanted to live in a compound. I wonder if any of these perfectly human houses with their perfectly human occupants knew who their neighbor was or what had been done in that house. I walked until I reached the end of the road. Absentmindedly, I touched the road sign. Passings Drive. How adequate.

"What is this supernatural show you keep thinking about?" Death whispered to me.

I just smiled but it was not full of joy and it was certainly not a pretty expression. I was focused on the tasks at hand and just stared at the phone in mine.

This was a number that I hadn't called in a long time. I stared at those numbers blinking at me from my phone. I took a deep breath, holding it in until it forcibly came out again. Continuously ignoring my ever growing shadow.

"Who is this and how did you get this number?" The voice was so familiar. Like I was still right by his side and never left. I said nothing. He quickly caught on to the old habit.

"Hi, Rhyd. It's been awhile." His voice lost some of the hostility. That phone call lasted a lot longer than it normally would have. I had to force my thoughts to stay behind a wall. Death didn't need to hear anything I thought about my first boyfriend. My only boyfriend.

"What can I do for you, doll face?"

I quickly outlined the past day and night to him. It was hard to believe I had only been involved in this for one day. He listened quietly until I was done. I avoided telling him too much about Death, he either wouldn't believe me or would be way too curious about her. I just didn't know who else to call. It's not like I could hit up dad with a phone call and have him rush over. I almost wish I could. He could see his two daughters back together and alive. Well, sort of. Dad would be so proud of Allison. I doubt he'd have any good words for me. But I would still be happy to see him.

Rylan helped me once Allison and dad died. Mom wasn't a hunter, there was nothing she could do here to help. She wasn't any help when I tracked down that wolf pack, she wasn't any help with any hunting. She just didn't know what to do. But it was all that I could do.

My ex took me under his wing. With everything I had learned from dad and anything I had picked up from him, I became one of the best hunters in the world. One of the few who made it past their fifth year in the business. But he had left me when there was a werewolf pack on his tail. I guess really I left him. I couldn't handle it if I had lost him, too. So I ran. It was one thing that I did very well. I made sure he was alive afterwards, though. I didn't know if he would ever forgive me. I didn't know if he waited for me. Of course, I knew he did. But for how long, I did not know.

But he agreed to help me. That was something, right? Even if it was to punch me for being a little sissy. I'd do the same if I was him. I'd take it. I deserved it. I had to ask Death where we were so he could find us. She did, if not a bit unwillingly. Wisconsin, of all places, near Blue Mounds, which made sense given where the compound was. But now it was time to help my sister and I'm not afraid to admit that I needed help. He's the best choice I have. Hell, he was the only choice that I have.

"It'll be real good to see you again, baby."

When I hung up the phone, Death's eyes still remained on me. I started to blush, thinking about his goodbye line. She didn't say a word. But I knew. I was jealous of a dead girl. I *dead* dead girl. Now she was jealous of a long dead love. We both have some issues, it seems. May the past kill our dreams, slowly but surely.

Rylan would be here in a day or two. In that time, who knew what would happen? There was nothing more for me to do out here. They all wanted to get me back inside as soon as possible, anyway. I don't think they understood that I wasn't the one in danger here. I don't know what we would do when we got back. We've already discussed it and I've seen the murder scenes. We had no other working theories. Just a lot of pieces to a puzzle that didn't fit together. I truly did not know what to do. And I didn't like it. I don't know what Allison was thinking. I couldn't do this. There were no real clues and no solid leads to go on.

This is the coldest case I think I have ever had the displeasure of working on. I ran my hand through my hair, probably for the millionth time. I tried to think of what I would do or why I was doing it if I was in the killer's shoes. They wanted to get at Death. Why would they choose these people? Why not go after Allison and Clark, the obvious, most dangerous targets? Maybe the killer isn't ready for that big of a mission yet. Maybe he's just trying to get Death's attention. Trying to draw her out for some reason or another. I growled as we walked. Death glanced at me but I didn't say a word. Nothing was going to touch her. I saw her lip twitch but just barely.

"Alright, hold on." I stopped walking and looked at Allison. "Take me back to my bike for a minute. I got some books in my saddlebags, maybe they can help."

Allison didn't even hesitate, she just grabbed me and we were gone.

"Oh, shi---" I nearly toppled over. Allison grabbed a hold of my arm to steady me. Then gently placed her fingers on my forehead, just like before. I blew out the breath I didn't realize I was holding.

"Okay, let me just grab these." I walked over to my bike, it was the only vehicle in the parking lot of this shithole. I staggered a bit, bracing myself against my bike. My saddle bags were old fashioned but they did the trick. I opened the flap and grabbed the only two books inside.

I closed it up and stretched, not looking back at my sister. "Any chance you'll let me drive back?"

When I was about to turn Allison grabbed my arm once again, "Nope." And we were gone again.

When we landed again, I stumbled into Death. She caught me and held on until I righted myself. She tried to do the finger trick but I stumbled back until it was Allison who caught me. I let her do it.

"Okay, thanks, never doing that again." I tossed my arm up, so Death would lead the way home. Off we went.

I had almost forgotten what had happened back there on the phone and with Death but she certainly didn't. Death must have been holding it in for a while. She didn't say a single word until we made it back to her personal cabin. I was very intimidated by the feeling radiating off of her. And all of a sudden, I didn't want to be alone with her. Death turned to me and walked forward until I felt the need to back up. Then she kept moving until I was backed against a wall. The only thing between us were the two books I held to my chest.

She looked at me, up and down. From my forehead to my lips to my shoes, to my eyes and back multiple times. It was the kind of look where you felt naked no matter how many layers you had on cause it went deeper than clothes, deeper than skin and bone and blood. It was the kind of look that sees your soul and makes your heart hiccup. I felt very uncomfortable. I opened my mouth to speak. But no words escaped me. I looked for a different escape route. Hair fell in my face. I looked at Death when she grabbed a piece, tracing my face and placing it back behind my ear where it was. I'm sure my eyes were big and round, making me look five years younger. Rylan had a name for that face but I didn't want to think about that or him right now. My mouth opened slightly out of nerves and my need to speak. I managed to maneuver myself around her and try to get away.

"She chose you because you *can* do this. You have no faith in yourself." Death had grabbed my hand so I couldn't get too far away and looked at it. I sat on the bed and Death followed me. I really didn't know how to respond to that. I ended up laying back on the bed and stared up at the ceiling, the books I once held fell to the ground. I hadn't noticed before but there was a tapestry hanging from the ceiling above the bed. It was surprising and made me smile for it was full of bright and lively colors.

No one would expect Death to like bright colors, or to care for her people so strongly, to hold the hand of a damaged girl, or to wear flowing dresses.

"Yes, I am often found as strange and unpredictable. It is very useful for people to underestimate you, Rhydian. Use it to your advantage."

I looked at her. She looked so normal. I looked her in the eyes. I still couldn't get over how beautiful they are. I wonder if she would feel the same. Like a normal girl. Taste the same. I brought my hand up and lightly grazed her lips before I could stop myself. Death just kept looking into my eyes.

My lips parted slightly as I leaned forward. I'd get close to her and backup again, slowly inching my way to her and she'd let me. She sat completely still, waiting for me to decide. I put my hand around the side of her neck and instead of moving closer, I pulled her into me. It was probably the lightest kiss I'd ever had. I pulled away after the chill of her lips started to burn.

"I'm sorry," we both said at the same time. All I did was think of how stupid an idea that was and who knew what was going to happen to me in the next couple of days and Death had her own things to worry about without needing to babysit me. I let her hear it all. It was so much easier than speaking.

"I am sorry I hurt you," was all Death said before exiting the room. I stood as she left and I just kept standing. I waited for only a couple more seconds before Death came back through the door and pulled me back into her arms, locking our lips together once again. I ignored the painful cold that came from her and held on for dear life.

I was wrong, she didn't taste like a normal girl. She tasted of flower petals and wine. I could get drunk off of her. My hands wrapped in her hair, pulling her closer, delighting in the cold burn. Death had one hand on my cheek and the other was fisted in the back of my shirt. Holding me in place.

I thought I heard footsteps but I was too distracted to care. I was getting out of breath and light headed. I pulled away ever so slightly to try to catch my breath. I swayed on the back of my heels. But we didn't let go of each other.

"Hey, Death, Al has to talk to you." I heard the voice and recognized it as belonging to Clark. I could not get myself to focus on it. I swayed back again before I collapsed. The last thing I remember was Death trying to catch me. I knew I hit the ground but I didn't feel it. I couldn't see anything. There was a feeling that people were hovering around above me. I thought I heard Allison's voice, she sounded concerned. I wasn't. I was very relaxed for the first time in a very long time.

I got to kiss Death and now I got to sleep. Why would I be concerned? I don't think I ever lost consciousness completely.

4 DOWN WITH THE WITCH

"What happened?" Yeah, that was Allison.

"I am not completely sure." Death. I thought it sounded like she was lying.

Are you alright? Her words whirled around my head. They felt like a warm blanket over my chilled mind. I could just imagine a little ice goat walking over my brain and her voice chasing it away.

I'm great. I tried to smile but I had no control over my body. It was like I was just in a hollow shell but I couldn't move the shell. Like a prison. Yeah, that sounds about right.

"What do we do?" I thought it was Clark but it could have been Allison again. Why do they need to do anything? I was completely fine here.

I could feel it when Death leaned over me and whispered in my ear, "I am so sorry." Her cool fingers pressed against my forehead. If I could have, I would have protested. No need of a repeat of the last time she did that to me. I truly believed I'd always subconsciously flinch away from her. My mind rolled that thought round for a minute, it tasted about right.

I opened my eyes almost immediately and sucked in a breath. It felt like I had been holding it for a while. I shot up and knocked my head straight into Allison's. I felt her take me in her arms. I looked over her shoulder at Death, she looked so guilty. *Please do not regret this.* I wasn't sure if she got the message but based on her making eye contact with me, I assumed she did. She didn't look like she was going to change her mind. I'm not even completely sure what had happened. But I do know it was caused by that kiss. And what a great kiss that was. I blew out a breath in a sigh.

I looked over at Clark. He was looking between the two of us just staring at each other. He didn't say a word but he looked suspicious. I had a strange feeling about this guy.

"What happened?" Allison pushed me far enough away that she could see my face and she examined it closely. Too closely. I pushed her farther back and slumped my shoulders. I was fine, I didn't need them all to hover over me.

"Not sure. I just felt really light headed and the next thing I knew, I was on the ground and you were all around me." I rubbed my forehead from where we hit each other. Then I let it linger on the place where Death had done her mojo on me. I don't know why we both lied about what happened. We may not know exactly what happened, but that wasn't the whole truth. We knew what caused it.

Allison rocked back on her toes and stood up. She didn't want to believe me but she knew not to push. She pulled me up by my forearms without difficulty even though I was at least double her size. Surprising, how much a person can change when they're not a person anymore. She leaned in close to whisper to me even though any reaper within fifty yards probably could have heard her, "Are you off your meds?"

I looked at her, shocked, I haven't been taking the antidepressant pills I was given since I had them really. They prescribed them but no one really understood so I didn't bother taking them. Then I realized what she was really talking about. My witch pills. When the witch fueled me up with her juice we were worried that there would be bad effects, and there were. I would start doing things differently, walking and talking and thinking. It showed in my hunting and it was not good. I became reckless, a little too eager for the kill. Like a rabid dog. Or a witch. I'd be putting everyone in my group directly into the line of fire. They were all in danger, and so was I. I would torture the evil we caught just for the hell of it. Until I wasn't much better than they were. I would become one of the very things we hunted for a living. If I really focused I could probably still create the lightning between my hands. I've been out of those pills for a while. Who knew what I could do now?

No bad effects have shown up so far but I had stopped hunting since I ran out. No high levels of stress or anger to push the witch out. I gave her a curt nod in response. Clark threw his hands up like he was tired of me already. She must have told him. I glared at him, he was getting on my nerves, as well.

"So not only is there a storm brewing outside and a psycho murderer on the loose but now we have a goddamn witch on our hands."

I was in front of him much faster than I remembered I could move. Looks like bringing up old memories brought some other things back, too. It was too fast but I didn't try to show the wobble that I felt in my knees. My head lulled to one side. I didn't try to push her back down.

"I am no witch." I made each word very clear and gritted them through my teeth. My eyes started to burn, probably the remnants of Death's kiss. I completely ignored the other things he listed.

We always ended up nose to nose and this was no different. "Not from where I'm standing." He spit the words at me. And I could see my reflection in his eyes. It looked like there were little flames dancing back in my own. My cheeks sunk a little and my skin became darker. I ignored it all. It's been far too long since I've felt like this. And it felt good. There was a fire burning in my veins. And I liked it.

He thrusted his arm out and I thought he was going to swing. I grabbed his arm and brought it down to my knee. It didn't break. I narrowed my eyes and twisted it so it was on his back at an awkward, and painful, angle. He threw his whole body against the wall, forcing me to let go. He faked a lunge towards me and I tackled him, that made us roll out of the door of the cabin, taking strands of beads with us. I tried to tear his throat out. I didn't have claws but I bet I could do it. He had to pull my hair back to keep me from succeeding.

We both fought to get the upper hand. He was on top of me. I was on top of him. And the wheel kept spinning round. Back and forth we'd go until we rolled one too many times and rolled right off the walkway. It was about a forty-eight foot drop. They should really invest in rails.

I maneuvered us so he would hit the ground and he did, taking most of the impact. I banged my head off the ground and I could already feel blood coming out. I ignored the fact that it was dark out even though it wasn't late enough in the day. I got up with only slight issues and lulled my head to look around. I would fight anyone near me. Maybe even Allison. Reapers were coming from different directions to see what just happened. I hoped one of them had an itch they needed me to scratch, too. I could feel the witch's magic moving through my veins. Consuming me.

I was moving like a rag doll. Stumbling around. It seemed at any moment any of my limbs would fall right off. But I was solid. "Has your training prepared you for me, reaper?"

They made a circle around me and I walked the edge of it. Looking at all of them, I'd reach out to touch a few and they'd back away. It made me laugh. Except it wasn't my laugh that came out. It sounded like some kind of twisted cackle. But I pouted. Looks like none of them wanted to play. They kept their distance, like I was a wild animal in a cage, yes. That is exactly what I was and I had just gotten loose. I heard Clark get up and I rolled my head across my shoulders to smile at him. I could feel my lip twitch. I had been hoping he was dead. Ah, but maybe he was still up for a game.

"Come on, big boy. Play with me." I rubbed my hands together to prepare for what I was going to try to do. I was confident. Like I had been doing this my whole life. I didn't think of any of the restraints I had only moments ago. No, now I was a different me. And I revelled in it. I noticed Allison and Death rushing down the ladders or floating down, trying to get to us. I paid them no attention.

I focused on my hands again, still rubbing them together. I slowly moved them apart and flickers of heat hit me. I called it to me. I tried harder, slowly moving my hands farther and farther apart. Little blue flames started floating in between. Dancing around my fingers. I didn't know I still had enough of the witch in me to do this. Guess I just needed a trigger. And I was staring at my loaded gun.

"Rhydian, stop!" I hadn't even begun yet, I ignored Allison's plea. It was time for me to play. Lightning had begun to crackle above us, I tilted my head. Was that from me? I smiled, hoping it was.

"Didn't they tell you not to play with fire as a kid?" I knew Clark was scared, he didn't know what to do. I didn't either but I knew what I wanted to do.

I felt my body move without even telling it to. My hips swayed and I danced around the circle, spreading fire everywhere I went. I didn't know what I was doing, must have been the witch instinct in me, telling me to move. There was a perfect circle of flame around us. I was fire and they were ice and I knew they wouldn't cross it. And right outside of it was a perfect ring of reapers. I spun over my shoulder and focused harder. I threw my hands towards Clark but nothing happened. Then a tree in the distance caught on fire. I frowned. That's not where I was aiming.

There was a blinding light that came from my left. I saw Clark in my peripherals advancing. I looked at the light and growled, crouching low. I heard a car door slam and a man's figure appear. I looked back at Clark. He was on me. He had my back pinned against him and my arms behind me. He held me by my throat. I tried to bite at his hand. I reached behind me in the most unnatural way and grabbed his head. He screamed. But he didn't let go. Neither did I. I started to panic. I could feel the fire spreading on my fingers but he still held on. I attempted to kick at his legs, trying to get him to release his hold. He was still screaming. He didn't budge.

"Death, do it now!" he screamed even louder, my flames were getting hotter, I could feel it. I started mumbling under my breath, calling it to me as much as I remembered I could. I didn't even see her coming. She was just in front of me, a hand on each side of my head. I hissed at the difference in temperature. I sucked air, fire cannot live without it and I felt that I was losing oxygen. I let go of Clark and placed my hands right over hers, she didn't even flinch although my hands were completely engulfed in flames. I screamed again. She didn't let go and I was choking on nothing, trying to keep my flames alive. Lightning cracked from above but even it was losing its strength. I looked at my hands and they had already begun to die out. I struggled and Clark just tightened his hold on my neck. I was freezing and soon there was no heat in me at all. I fell to my knees and they both let me go, backing up.

"What the hell's going on here?" Rylan pushed his way into the crowd, my ring of fire disappeared with my hot hands. I tried to laugh but it sounded like sandpaper against a brick wall. I said the same thing the first time I saw a fighting ring here. He fell to his knees alongside me, although it was more graceful and willing, wrapping me in his arm. He pulled a gun out with the other hand and moved it between Death and Clark because they were the only two near me, not knowing which one would cause the most trouble. Finally, it landed on Clark which was very sexist, and if I was in my right mind I·would have given him an earful about it. But since Death moved ever so closer, he switched to her.

"Babe, what's going on?" He still didn't know who to aim at though bullets wouldn't do any good at the moment, not here. I looked at him when he called me babe but I couldn't figure out why it mattered that he didn't say that. It was getting harder to focus. I was so cold. I wanted to be warm again. I glanced up. I wanted to fight him again.

I cackled once more. I found all of this too amusing and hoped some more destruction would really start to happen. Guns were way too much fun. I raised my hand up to touch it but Rylan kept me against him so I couldn't reach it. He knew me too well. But he was warm so I stayed against him.

"Look at her, man. You tell me." That was Clark. Rylan did look at me then. He took a good hard look in my eyes and he knew. He cursed under his breath but he still held me against his chest.

Rylan scooted only slightly away from me so we were face to face. And then he kissed me. Right there in front of everyone. There was a snap like a rubber band in my head and I leaned closer into him before pushing him away from me. I raised my hand to slap him but he caught it. I tried again with my other hand and he grabbed that one, too.

"That's my girl." He said it with a smile. He brushed the hair away from my now sweaty face, releasing one of my hands. I didn't try to hit him again. I don't know why I didn't try to hit him this time. "Why didn't you go get more pills?" He knew the story. He's seen me in the worst place of my life and he's seen me as the worst witch he's ever come across. And he still came back for me.

"I quit the life. I didn't need them anymore. I haven't had an episode since I ran out. Well, until now. I guess I was just triggered." My voice was dry and I had to clear my throat several times to even say that much. I glared at Clark once I was done.

Rylan followed my eyes. He raised his gun and once again pointed it at Clark.

"You did this to her?" Rylan stood up, bringing me up with him. Allison came to stand by Clark's side. Death stepped between us all.

I tapped Rylan's chest and made a motion with my hand. Our own silent sign language. He lowered his gun once again and he put his hand on my face. My cheek resting in his palm. He moved slowly toward me, giving me plenty of time to pull away or tell him no. I let him come and he lightly pressed his lips to mine then he pressed them to my forehead.

"It's damn good to see you, Rhyd." He wrapped me in his arms once again.

I whispered in his ear, "You should have killed me when you had the chance."

He pulled away and just stared at me. When we met I was close to giving into my witchy ways. He was hunting me and I almost killed him. I would've killed him, too, but something stopped me. Something stopped him. That's how we met. That's how our paths have become intertwined. He could see all those memories running through my head, as I'm sure they were running through his. He just kissed my forehead again. I could feel the warmth spread through me, my skin slowly returning to normal along with my eyes.

Rylan let go of me and looked at Allison. He smiled. “And you must be little Ally I’ve heard so much about.” He went in for a hug but based on the gun still being in his hand she didn’t budge. He put it back in his holster and stuck his hand out for her to shake instead. She didn’t take it either.

“You’re the one who saved my sister.” Allison didn’t sound very pleased with the idea. I could tell she didn’t like him but I didn’t like Clark, so we were even.

Thunder cracked across the sky again. It was blue and looked like electricity tracing its way through the world.

“What the hell?” I looked over at Death. It appeared she was pointedly not making eye contact with me.

“Hey.” She looked, I pointed up at the sky, “ What is this? I’ve never created anything like that before. It’s not from me.”

She nodded and began to walk away. I didn’t even see when her goat came up but it was now walking beside her. “I am aware.”

And she was gone. Death raised up into the sky and disappeared. I looked back at Allison, throwing my arms out. She shrugged her shoulders.

"She knows something." I went to follow her, Rylan just behind me.

Allison stopped me. I went to push past her. Clark stepped up and I glared at him again. Rylan pointed his gun at Clark's head. Now that would kill him.

"We have better things to do than kill each other. No matter how much I'd like to do that." I pushed Rylan's hand down. I held on to it and led him towards the war room. It was more like a council hall but whatever they want to call it is their business. That's where everything is that involves the case. I explained all of this to Rylan on our way there. I had only just heard about it so I haven't made it in to see it yet either. Allison and Clark were right behind us. A very literal right, I could feel them breathing and I could feel Al holding the tiger cat back there at bay.

"How'd you get here so quickly? I wasn't expecting you until at least tomorrow." I tried to be quiet but it wouldn't have mattered, they could still hear us.

"I never told you where I was, I was already real close and the job didn't last as long as I thought it would. I came straight here from that. Only took me a couple hours."

"I'm glad it did." I mumbled. I could feel him smile but he didn't say anything further on the matter.

The war room is just an empty room, except for a big round table in the middle. The walls were made out of corkboard except for one in the corner that was dry erase. Everything you need to figure out who a murderer was. I just hoped in the end it would be Clark so I could kill him myself. A little ting went off in my head like I was onto something, like I should be remembering something. I looked at Clark and tilted my head. No, it couldn't be him. He wasn't smart enough.

I shook my head and leaned against the table. I was angled towards the board with all the victims faces on it. "It would have to be an inside job. None of them lived on the compound. They didn't have the same circle of friends. Didn't have the same enemies. The only thing in common is that they are reapers. There's nothing else for us to go off of."

Death made it mandatory for all reapers to now live on the compound. Whether it made it easier or harder for the killer, I guess we'll find out. But it was a good reason for them to come. No need for anyone else to get killed alone. And so far nobody has died since the great migration. We have no new evidence to work with. I've never wanted someone to die so much in my life. I sighed. I shouldn't be such a Debbie downer about this. We have suspects but of course, they are not panning out.

I looked up when Rylan tapped me on the shoulder with something warm. It was coffee. I jumped up to grab it. I felt like I had been in the war room, staring at the same board for days. In reality, I had been.

"Where did you find this?" He smiled. He knew exactly how to cheer me up.

"You didn't know? Death brought a bunch of stuff in for you since you've had to scrounge otherwise."

I blushed. I knew she got some things but I didn't know the extent of it. "Well, you need stuff, too. So it's not just for me."

He gave me a look. "You were here first and most of this stuff was already here. It's not for me."

"Well, it's for us now." I took a sip and closed my eyes at the fullness of warmth it gave me. I held it close to my chest and looked back up at him.

"Thank you." I knew I didn't need to say the words but I chose to do it anyway.

"I still cannot believe that Death is real. I mean, hunters talked about it, but you never really believe those types, you know?"

I smiled. I did know. "I felt the same way when I got here, lucky for you your welcome was a lot better than mine." I made a face and he laughed.

Rylan nodded. He pulled a chair up next to me in front of one of the boards and looked. "What's going on between you two? I see the way she looks at you."

I put my knees to my chest and placed my cup on top of them, resting my cheek against my thighs. "I don't know," which was the truth. I had no idea what she was thinking. "There's just a pull, you know. I can't help but want to be near her, I think she feels it, too. But it's dangerous. She hurts me." I saw Rylan stiffen, I quickly shook my head, "Not like that, it's her power. She feels terrible about it, it's not her fault. I'm sure it's equally my fault with the witch's juju in me. Fire and ice don't tend to mix."

Rylan placed a hand on my knee. "Just follow your heart." It was the most cliche, stupidest thing I've ever heard him say. I could tell he thought the same. For a second I let my mind wonder what would happen if it led me back to him.

"That thing is stupid and doesn't know what it wants." I stood up and paced back and forth in front of the victim board.

I stopped and stared at all the pictures looking back at me. I stopped and stared at all those souls that were lost for nothing. I stopped and stared at all those victims and thanked whatever god was out there that my sister wasn't one of them. I turned back to Rylan. He had moved over to sit on the makeshift bed we set up for him. He wasn't comfortable sharing a room with a reaper and there wasn't really space anywhere else. I looked away.

Start from the beginning. "It has to be an inside job."

"Alright. You already said that, though. I agree but tell me why like I don't."

"I've been reading into some of the books that my dad left behind," they were sitting on the table and I flipped a few pages and slid it over to him, "There are no weapons that can take souls out of existence, however, it is possible for reapers to do it. They have to collect souls from bodies so it only makes sense that they are able to destroy them as well."

I thought about it for a second. “There’s no way any one of these reapers were into anything bad enough that it got them killed in the exact same way. So it’s the same killer. The killer would have had to have known their schedules. They play and hang out during the day. They work at night. They don’t need to sleep or eat. He would’ve had to know that these specific reapers did not live on the compound. So he needed to know intimate details about their lives and none of them had the same friends because they are different people. So Death is right it has to be about revenge. But why? What did she do to this thing?”

I took a breath and continued. “We don’t even have any real clues to what this thing could be except for this. And I have never read or heard about anything else that has powers over souls. That would explain why everyone’s been so secretive about the whole thing. They know it’s another reaper, they just don’t know who or what it has to do with Death. We don’t even know if this thing is after her, in the first place.” I started pacing again.

Rylan walked in front of me and grabbed me by the shoulders so I couldn’t continue to move. Curse him. That was the best way for me to think.

"Alright, that's good. Now we need to find out why he chose these reapers. What do these reapers mean to her? Who would know all this information?"

"Well, Death, me, Allison, Clark, and you. But Allison is the one who came and got me so it's neither of us, you arrived after the deaths started, Death has been with me when murders occurred, and Clark is too stupid for this amount of planning."

I thought about his other questions. "The last one that was killed was a brand new reaper. She just made her. I think one of them was the first reaper she ever made. I'm not sure about the others. Maybe lovers or good friends or they knew each other in their before life or, "I cursed, I didn't know, there were too many routes to look through,"Besides, it could be any number of the reapers, I haven't met all of them. JUst the victim's friends and family. It could be anything. Any reason. He doesn't even have to have a reason. And if he does, why wouldn't he come after Allison or Clark? Those are her two best warriors, her trainers. Without them, she would have to start all over again."

"Maybe it's one of them." I looked at him like he was crazy.

"Please, my sister would never do such a thing."

"You don't know your sister like you used to. She's a different person now. You're a different person now."

I shook my head. "No, it's not her."

I sat on the table and got right back up, I felt useless. I've only been working for a couple of days but I have nothing. Absolutely nothing to go on. "Okay, what about Clark again, then?"

I was prepared to think many ungodly things about Clark but it didn't feel right. "He doesn't have the balls." Rylan laughed.

"Who doesn't have the balls?" Clark walked into the room.

I was in a defensive stance immediately and Rylan had his gun out already. Clark put his hands up in a sign of surrender. I called bullshit.

"What do you want?" It was more of a hiss but it was better than just attacking him. At least, I stopped to ask. No one can say I didn't try to take the high road.

"We come bearing gifts." That was Allison, she gracefully came out from behind Clark holding a basket of something. Then I could feel it. It was cold and I laughed. The basket was a makeshift cooler. And as she walked closer I could peak what was inside. It was a basket full of beer. I prefered whiskey but I wasn't going to complain.

"I'm sorry for earlier. We've all been super stressed about the cases and one thing led to another." Clark didn't move from the door.

I nodded, "Don't worry, I'm not sorry, either." I looked back over to Allison, "Did we ever figure out what that storm was?"

"It's called a Dark Cloud. It is pretty much a storm full of supernatural creatures." Death floated through the door this time. Literally floated, that is. I ignored it to glare at the goat. Little snitch. I don't like snitches.

"Dark Cloud? That's a real creative name."

"This is not something to be joked about. This is not a game."

"Sure, it is, sweetheart. And we're losing it." I kept glaring at the goat, maybe one of those supernatural creatures were big enough to swallow that thing whole.

"Out," and just like that, Death called her goat away and it ran,I don't know where.

"There haven't been any more deaths, I have no idea what you think I can do to help you, at this point. But go ahead and tell me more. Maybe it has something to do with this whole situation."

"In fact, it does, there is a door that unlocks this storm. It is the killing of reapers. But the sacrifices are not done yet. There have only been five murders. There needs to be two more. Then the full wrath of Hell will be upon us."

It sounded so fake, we all just stood there and stared at her. What were we supposed to say? 'Nah, you're just playing with us', I would love to see anyone say that to Death.

"I understand your skepticism, even to my own ears it does not seem realistic. But it is very real and it is happening and I need to protect my reapers while you catch the killer. The door to the Cloud has long been forgotten. Someone has found it and we need to find out how."

"And where do you expect us to figure that out at?" Rylan put his gun away.

"That, Rylan, is simple," Death began to walk out of the building, we scrambled to follow her. "To the library."

5 OH WISE ONE

Out of all the things, that was not what I expected her to say. Maybe go back to the crime scenes again or reinterview the witnesses or go somewhere else. Not to a library. I didn't even know there was a library on the compound. I haven't explored all of it yet but I suspected that if there was a library that I would have noticed.

I shouldn't have been surprised. There were always a lot of books scattered all over Death's room. I looked at a few but they were all in Latin. And though I have a great many talents, reading Latin is one of them, but I do not like it. You can't survive as a hunter if you can't at least read and speak Latin, writing it helps but not as needed as the others. You would die and be killed so many times over. But books, they'll save your life more times than one. Even if you have to just throw them, which I have.

I asked her about it the other night. Why she had a bunch of half-finished books scattered around her floor, why they were all in Latin. She said it makes her feel her age. There hasn't been another Death in at least a millenia. I believed her. Considering half the hunting population didn't even believe that she existed, I can't imagine the job switching hands very often. That wouldn't be able to stay under our radar for very long. I liked the image of Death sprawled out on her round bed with her feet kicked up with a book that was older than me in her hands, looking like a rowdy teenager.

It didn't take too long to get to the library. I guess everyone knew where it was, just nobody wanted to go there. And they say our youth isn't learning. Looks like our dead weren't either. We had to go through the woods to get to it. It was on the outskirts of the compound, cliffside. Technically, the entire woods were a part of the compound. It's not like there was a fence keeping us in. Or anybody else out.

There was a path and it led us to the other side of the cliff. I still think of how easy it would be to just jump, to leave this problem to everybody else. The line of us was forced to a stop and Death dropped in front of me, she was the one leading the convoy.

"How did yo.." Death shoved me against the closest tree, choking me with her forearm. Rylan pulled his gun but Allison stepped between him and Death. Maybe if he would've gone for a knife, like I did, he would've made it. My knife was placed against Death's gut. It wouldn't kill her but it would certainly leave a scar.

"Don't you even think about it. Do you hear me?" I saw Rylan focus his gun on Allison instead of Death, Clark pushing her out of the way, and then Allison coming to try and pry Death off of me. "They may not be able to hear your thoughts but I still can," she looked as if she wanted to cry, "I can." That is when she released me and just kept walking.

Clark followed her immediately, Allison hesitantly behind him. I fell to my knees, choking to get air back in. Rylan helped me up, I pushed him off and began to follow the procession. Rylan at my back. I kept the knife in my hand, it solidified me. Calmed me down.

She led us to a set of stairs carved into the side of the cliff. If we wouldn't have just had an episode, I would have been awed by the craftsmanship of them. They truly were a work of art. I looked behind me. There were gods carved into the bottom half of each stair, depicting a different event in history. I recognized Cleopatra, and the battle of Troy, Pompeii. I didn't know how exactly I knew they were gods but I did. And they looked magnificent.

At the bottom of the stairs, there was a flat little place that led to a mouth of a cave. It was less like a cave and more like the cliff stopped and a cover was created like a porch. There was water trickling down from the rocky structure. The grass hanging down had begun to turn black. The storm is already beginning to affect the land around us. We walked forward into the dark cave that wasn't like a cave. Lights flickered on as we approached the door. And it was a giant piece of art itself. It looked like it was made of redwood. Carved with an intricate design that brought about images of kilts and red hair and thick accents. Gorgeous.

"I know." Death said from the front.

It opened with a creak without anyone touching it. I had the feeling it only did that for Death, leaving the rest of us to have to shove it open. And by the grinding of the hinges against the stone, I could tell that it would be heavy far before I laid a hand on it. I was right.

We followed behind like waddling geese behind our mother. Death *was* oddly mother-like. She led us into a dimly lit room. I could tell in a heartbeat that this was now going to be my favorite place on the compound. My mouth fell open with amazement that the stairs and the door couldn't quite entice.

This library was two stories. Sort of. The first floor had a high ceiling which means that the second floor ceiling hung very low. The boys would be very uncomfortable up there but I could see how it would be completely fine for us girls.

Everywhere around us were bookcases, each with at least six shelves. Some had more, higher levels. There was a rolling ladder pressed against the shelf nearest to us. Everywhere you looked there were books and I fell in love almost instantly. All the cases and the wooden mold around the ceiling were a dark wood. Not as dark as the door but not very light either. I didn't quite recognize the wood.

The staircase leading up to the second floor was narrow and the ceiling above it was domed upward. There was a desk in the front half of the little room and in the back half was a table. From where I stood it looked like there was another one upstairs. The desk closest to us had a fairly large statue of an owl. A perfect overseer for a library, it made me smile. It was also made of wood. So delicately carved. Every detail was just right and necessary. I could just imagine this bird ruffling its feathers. Spreading its wings to search the library for any knowledge it seeked.

"That statue." I pointed it out to Death, like she didn't already know that it was there.

She nodded and smiled, "That is, in fact, who we came to see."

I looked back at Death, confused. I glanced behind me to where Rylan and Allison stood. When I glanced back over, the owl had moved. Now that would not have impacted me at all, except for the fact that none of us were near where it was.

Leaning, I raked my gaze over the owl once again, moving closer to it. I knelt down til I was about eye level with it. And it blinked. I stumbled back, quickly enough that I fell over. I rushed to my knees again and stuck a hand out to touch it, to make sure it was still made out of wood. The owl stood up to its full height, out of its crouch.

I hesitantly kept my hand out. I lightly touched it's wooden feathers, I could feel that they were all individually made and not just one piece. They felt so real but I was not mistaken. It was still made out of wood.

"How is this possible?" It was more of an awed statement than a question.

The bird leaned its little head toward me and opened its beak. “Magic.”

“Holy shit. It can talk!” My mouth fell open and I smiled. I knew magic existed, obviously. But I hadn't seen much of it. Not positively at least. This was simple. And innocent. And beautiful. I laughed at the beauty of it. I covered my mouth with a hand but it did nothing to hide my girlish smile.

“Of course I can talk.” The owl flew over to land on Death’s shoulder. I stood up and followed it. I didn’t want to let it out of my sight. I thought it was wonderful and I always wanted to be around it. Pure magic. Not black magic. I’ve never seen anything like it.

“That’s the effect good magic is supposed to have on you.” Death said, once again reading my mind. It didn’t bother me this time.

“Ah, so you are the special girl, then. The witchling.” It was the bird.

“I’m Rhydian.” It was all I could manage to say, I was still dumbfounded and have never been called a witchling before. At least he didn’t make it sound like a bad thing.

The owl flew over and landed on my shoulder this time. “Oh, yes, Madam Death. I see what you mean. She has it coursing through her veins, alright.”

He kind of hopped around until he was facing me, which was a bit awkward to have a bird's beak close to your eye but I found myself trusting this one. I couldn't even tell myself why.

"I am Martin, overseer of this library. Tell me, special girl, how did you acquire so much black magic? Or better yet, how has this much not killed you already? Or even better, how'd you manage that and still be so lighthearted in the presence of pure magic?"

I looked down and lifted my eyelashes just enough to see Death. "It's a long story."

"I rather like long stories, madam."

Death gathered the others around her. "Come, we have work to do. I believe this is a conversation better left to themselves." And they scattered. Death must have been talking to them in their heads because they all looked like they knew what they were looking for. It made me pout a little, not being the only one she would speak to in such a way.

Martin flew away again. I followed him. He led me to a little alcove off to the side of the back room. I hadn't noticed it in my initial sweep of the room. The little space was enclosed in cushions. It reminded me of a padded cell. I was supposed to be in one once upon a time. Rylan saved me from that. I glanced over at him. All I saw was his back. He was reaching for a book on a high shelf. He lifted it with ease, knowing his careless tendencies, I was worried for the book.

"Ah, but he cared for you, did he not? And I am rather inclined to believe that you, my dear, are much more fragile than any of my books." Martin had laid his perch on the other side of our cushioned shell. I leaned against the back wall of it so we were more next to each other rather than acrossed. I had a good view of Rylan from here, too.

"That he did." It didn't bother me that this bird, Martin, could obviously read my mind as well. For some reason, it didn't seem as intrusive than when Death did it.

"And yet you care for her, too. After only knowing her for such a short period of time. A trusting soul, you are."

I laughed. "No, actually. Not usually. Trust is to be earned. Not freely given. It just takes less for some than others."

"It took almost a year for you to trust that boy you keep staring at. You admire him. You trust him. You love him."

I knew I should probably deny it but he could already read my mind. No use in hiding from Martin. "I do."

"Then why, may I ask, are you not with him?" I laughed again, this was the question he asked permission on. He didn't even ask that about peeking into my mind.

"My apologies, madam." Martin bowed after that. As much as an owl could, at least.

"It's alright. Um," I stopped looking at Rylan to make eye contact with this mysterious, oddly open bird, "I'm not the same person I was when we were together the first time. A lot of things happened that I couldn't cope with anymore and I ran from him."

"And yet he is here. And you still love him. He still loves you. Oh, how do you kids say it these days? Oh yes. What is the problem?"

That made me laugh. I glanced back over at Rylan. He was already looking at me. He winked and gave a little wave with a sly smile. I waved back. I brought my knees up to my chest and rested my cheek on it. Looking back at Martin, "I guess I'm still running."

"Everything's moving too fast. In this case. In my life. With Death. With Rylan. And Allison and Clark. I just don't know what to do all the time. Or at all. And they expect me to be able to do all these things and I know I can't do them but I know what I do well.

There's one thing. And I do it very very well. Without fault."

"And what is that, special girl?"

"Run."

Death appeared then and whispered something in Martin's ear so low even my supernatural hearing couldn't catch it.

"I understand." Martin looked over at me, "I am afraid they are in need of my assistance and that there has been a development in your case."

Death stood up to her full height, and everyone was gathered in behind her, "It's time to go."

We filed out in the same order we came in. I was the last to leave. I was pulling the door shut when Martin spoke once again. "Oh, and Rhydian." I looked up. He was in the rafters, "I would still love to hear that story of yours. I do love a good story." I smiled.

"You can count on it," and closed the door. It made a very final click.

I leaned against the coolness of the wood. I closed my eyes. This was the one place that I felt safe. I don't know if it was because of a wooden bird or all the pure magic floating around in there. But it was safe. And we needed a lot of safe right now.

They were all waiting for me at the top of the stairs, letting me take my time like another murder didn't just happen. I climbed the stairs carefully, staring at the blackened grass, wishing I could just stay in the library with Martin for forever. I couldn't tell you how many times I looked back thinking I could just hide away in there. But life must move on, and so must death.

I reached the top of the steps and they were all staring at me. "I like those thoughts a lot better than your other ones." I knew exactly what she was talking about. I didn't say a word. I kept walking. This time, they all followed behind me.

The walk back to the camp was a quiet one. I tried to enter through the clearing but Death stopped me.

"No, no, love. We are going straight to the scene." She held her hand out to me and I sighed. I walked over to her and placed my arm in hers. Allison grabbed onto Rylan's arm.

I looked back at him as we all started to run towards a tree. "Just keep running. And Rylan?"

He looked at me, confused and nervous. He saw what we were running towards. "Yeah?"

"Take a deep breath." That's when I hit the tree with Death. Just like before we went right through it. I could hear Rylan groan, preparing for impact. Then he let his breath loose when he saw what happened to Death and I. He really should not have exhaled. I don't know why they choose to run before teleporting sometimes but not others, but I certainly appreciated it more than standing still.

Just as I expected, when Rylan came out, he was disoriented and he threw up. Death told me it affected us all differently but for most humans, Rylan's reaction is what happened. I was one of the few she's met who hasn't done that. Lucky me. I was a little winded but for the most part, unaffected. Looks like my body was finally getting used to jumping through space and time.

I held Rylan against a tree and made little circles on his back with my palm. I didn't want any of them to touch him. There are too many things that could go wrong with the touch of a reaper. Allison did step forward to do what she had done to me. I stepped in front of Rylan. We all knew I was different, who knew what would happen to him with that touch. Very similar to my first day here. I was protecting what was mine just like she did once upon a time. She nodded, understanding.

"Take deep breaths, Ry." I kept myself between him and everyone else.

"None of us want to hurt him, sister."

"I don't care. I'm tired of things getting taken away from me. This is mine and no one's going to touch him." I could feel the burn returning to my eyes. I let it come. I wanted to feel safe. I wanted to go back to the library. I wanted to go back to where my sister was alive and dad was alive. I wanted to protect my loved ones. Too many negative feelings. It's too much.

"Rhyd, I'm okay. They're not going to hurt me." I didn't care.

I looked at him. He swore under his breath. I heard it, as clear as day. He slowly brought his hands up to my shoulders. I flinched away from him but he kept creeping towards me. His hands were very gentle. At first. Once he latched onto me, he spun me around and slammed me against the same tree he was once leaning on.

"Get off me." I didn't know who I wanted to hurt. But I wanted it to happen. I looked at everyone around me. My eyes rested on Clark for a moment, I saw him tense up. But I kept going until I landed on Death. Now that would be a close fight.

I pushed away from Rylan. I knew I was stronger than him. It wouldn't even be hard. His feet were digging into the ground as we were slowly getting away from the tree. It was like a game of tug-a-war, except I needed to push instead of pull. And I did. I kept pushing.

"Al, don't." I could hear Clark's voice but I didn't look over. I wrapped my hand around Rylan's and stopped pushing, I let him push me against the tree. I wasn't anywhere I didn't want to be.

I screamed. It felt like ice was enclosing my arm. I looked down and saw that Allison had a hold on my wrist. She was leaning her way towards me because Clark was holding her back by the waist. She tightened her grip. I screamed again.

I let go of Rylan and placed my hand on top of hers. Something inside me told me that I didn't want to do it but a bigger part snuffed the little voice out. I laughed and saw fire coming out of my finger tips. Fire soon engulfed my hand. Allison let go with a yelp of pain. She fell back, into Clark.

I leaned into Rylan and licked his neck. "Mmm, yummy." I whispered in his ear. I jumped up so my legs were wrapped around his waist. And I kissed him. Hard and passionate. He got distracted, letting go of my neck in favor of my hips. I laughed again, swinging myself around so I was on his back. I bent over backwards and placed my hands on the ground. Walking on them, I let go of Rylan and headed towards Death. Doing a cartwheel, I placed my feet back on the ground and twisted and lowered myself until I was kneeling on the ground, facing her.

"Hiya, sugar. Is it time to play yet?" I crawled towards her. She didn't back away. I wasn't scared of her touching me, either. Both of my arms were engulfed in flames now.

"Yes, love. It is time to play." When I got to her, she picked me up by the shoulders. We were face to face.

"He's mine." I don't know why that was the one thought that kept wrapping itself around my head but it was. Something whispered to me. *He's yours. You can't let them take him. Protect what is yours. You don't like to share with others, remember?*

"I know." Death did the same trick Rylan did and shoved me against a tree. My head lulled back and I smiled.

"Let's play rough, then." I leaned in very close to her and nibbled at her neck. Then I bit into it. Hard.

I could taste blood but I didn't stop. It didn't disgust me like I thought it would. I held on like a dog with a bone and she didn't even try to stop me. I could see Rylan staring at me in horror. Clark with disgust. And Allison was crying out to me.

"Rhydian, stop! Please, you're hurting her!"

"No, she is not." Death spoke up even though I was canines deep in her throat. I could feel her move a hand from my shoulder and lose it in my hair. I felt it when she pulled on a handful. It made me open my mouth with a moan. I bit my lip and looked at her. Waiting to see what she'd do next.

"That is enough, love." She placed her forehead against mine. "That's enough."

I could feel my eyes roll backwards. My entire body was being enclosed in a chill. I couldn't move. Everything stood still. I started to shake and when I began to fall, Death was there to catch me. She was the only one unafraid of me. And I think just because she saw Rylan do it, she kissed me. Both of us were covered in her blood and could feel electricity go through me until it reached my brain and snapped. I took a deep breath and started coughing like I had been stuck under a sheet of ice in a frozen lake. I looked around like I didn't quite know where I was.

But I knew where I was. I knew what I was doing. I was that little voice on the inside and I shoved it out of existence. I tried to push Death away from me. I hurt her. I could've killed her. Death kissed me again. Pressing me closer to her, one hand still in my hair, the other on the small of my back. I stopped fighting. I slumped into her. Letting her support my weight.

"I am yours, as well." Death whispered in my ear when she pulled away.

I pushed her head away enough to look into her eyes. "I am so sorry." I tried to look at her neck but all I saw was blood.

6 MOUSETRAP

That was all I got to see. From all around us, reapers showered from every tree. I was stupid. I had some of the best senses in the world and I completely ignored what they were telling me. All because I was in a fiery haze. Death held onto me and separated me from everyone else. Rylan came over and stood by us. They knew why they were all here. I didn't. I guess it was kind of obvious now though.

"She's coming with us." Clark came up and went nose to nose with Death.

"She's nothing but a danger to all of us." I think that was Mave.

"She could be the killer." I don't know where that one came from.

But I could see Allison standing with the group of them, looking down, ashamed. They had us surrounded and I felt arms grabbing me. Death stood aside. Rylan tried to fight but there were far too many of them for the two of us.

"You know she is not the killer. I know she is not the killer. There has not been a second of her being here that I was not personally with her or my eyes were watching for me."

"So tell them to let me go." I struggled against the three people who had me.

"I cannot protect you from yourself." Death lightly touched my face. I hissed at the chill it left behind, my skin still hot from my fire. I could hear Rylan trying to fight. The burn never left my eyes.

"Let him go!" Death lifted her chin slightly. They released him. He stumbled over to me. One of them must have kicked him in the knee. He wasn't walking right. Cheap shot. And normally three guys couldn't have taken him on.

"Rhyd, I wasn't for this, at all. I didn't know what they were planning on doing." I looked straight through him.

"Run, and run fast. You're not going to want to be near this." He touched my face in the same place Death did. Now my skin was burning and he flinched at his now scorched fingers, "Go!"

He did. He kept looking back. Too soon he stopped and waited. He expected me to be able to run away with him. I wasn't so sure. I noticed several of the group of reapers run away with my warning, as well. Allison and Clark went up in the trees, as did Death. It would destroy me if I hurt them. I glanced up. More reapers were getting closer and closer to me. I was completely surrounded.

"It's a trap!" Rylan shouted.

It was unnecessary since I could see that. I was unafraid. They had to hold him back just as much as they did me. He would never let me go at it alone. He just might have to this time.

Because this time the fire started in my hair. That must have been a hell of a sight. I had a mane of wild flames and it was about to get even hotter.

I could feel something crawling underneath my skin. It felt like goosebumps but deeper down, embedded deep into my skin. I looked down at my hands and saw that something black was being traced throughout my veins.

No, not something. That was magic. Black magic. It was coursing through my veins. I watched it shoot up my arm. I could feel it painfully tracing its way up my throat. I stretched my neck in an attempt to get away from it. I actually screamed when it was on my face. Or rather, in my face. It should have scared me. Witch's veins were black. I knew my skin would grow dark but I never expected this. It didn't seem to matter now. The pain was over. I let out a breath, sagging slightly into my captors arms, which had significantly loosened.

The fire grew and grew, encasing my skin but not really touching me. No one dared get any closer to me. I'm sure I looked horrifying and I'm sure the facts weren't all that much better. A hunter who looks like a witch and knows far too much about killing reapers. I was their nightmare come to life.

Reapers had begun to back away. Black magic was a funny thing like that. There's usually so much in your body that it forces your body to evolve. Some people grow fatter, some grow things. Wings, tails, fangs and claws. Any number of abnormalities can be accounted for by witchcraft. But I wasn't a practitioner. This shouldn't be happening to me. I only started getting scared when I felt the same tingling that was in my veins run down my back. I lied, the pain was only beginning.

I hoped to god I wasn't about to sprout out a tail. Reapers had let go of me. Some began to run, others just backed away slowly, not sure of what was happening or what to do.

I felt myself becoming engulfed in flames. Those didn't hurt. Whatever was happening to my back did, though. I fell to my knees, screaming. I could see reapers and Rylan covering their ears.It was bloodcurdling.

I rolled onto my side and tried to curl up as much as possible. It felt like someone was trying to claw their way out of my spine from the inside.

"Rhydian!" I could hear Rylan start to run back towards me. I lifted myself onto my elbows. Just enough to see him.

Death flew down in front of him. "You need to stay back."

"You need to help her."

Death shook her head. "Those flames are the only thing not killing her. She's evolving," Death looked back at me, I met her eyes for a moment then I had to close mine with a scream, "And it's going to be painful. There is nothing I can do for her but wait."

He didn't know what to do. Being torn between helping me and killing himself. "Oh, Rhydian, tell me what to do, baby."

Rylan fell to his knees and crawled over to me. He sat right outside of my ball of fire. I could hear bones in my back cracking, and reshaping themselves. I was being twisted in every which way. I could feel whatever it was clawing its way out, breaking through the skin. I was beginning to lose my vision. I buried my face in the cool earth beneath me. I think the fire was the only thing keeping me conscious. I knew what was coming. I didn't want them. I liked to run. I didn't need to fly. No. No. No.

It felt like hours. And not so soon enough, it was over. I sagged into the earth, trying to catch my breath. My back felt heavy, being dragged down by the weight of body parts that weren't there moments ago. I tried to push myself up and only made it to my elbows before I had to stop to breathe. I saw Allison try to come to my aide but Clark held her back. Taking in a deep breath, I tried again.

I knelt up, taking big, deep, even breaths. I kept my eyes closed so the world wouldn't spin. Finally I looked up and stretched everything out. I flapped them harder and harder trying to get the new muscles to work where there once were none. I tried to get them to pick me up. I placed my feet on the ground after some time. My fire, mostly gone. Just lingering on my fingers and I could feel them on my new attachments. I stumbled forward. I kept turning around in a circle, trying to figure out where they went.

Like a dog chasing his tail, trying to figure it out.

I reached a hand back and grabbed a hold of one. I thought it would feel leathery or maybe would have feathers but neither was the case. It was soft, like a butterfly would be. But strong. Durable. These bad boys weren't going to break. I couldn't stop touching them, running my hands over every inch that I could reach. The veins felt sharp, almost like rope compared to what was holding them all together. What exactly was the anatomy of a wing called?

I stopped when I was facing Death. I heard a whistle from behind me, though. I turned around again to look at Rylan. I could feel the new bones, waving with my movements. My eyes no longer burned but the rest of me did. A peek down told me that my veins were still black, though.

"Wow." Death spoke. I backed up so I could see them both. And they were both staring at me.

"What?" I threw my hands out and fire hit a couple trees. I pulled my hands back into my chest. "Sorry." I mumbled. My new limbs folded just as my arms did. I could feel them mold themselves into my skin. Not gone but not out either.

"Your wings appear as tattoos on your back when at rest." Death stated. She seemed impressed with it. I didn't really have any say in the matter. I reached behind me and felt the back of my shoulder.

"Wow." I whispered more to myself than anybody else around me. There were still reapers there to take me in. I ignored them. My back felt like the veins of a leaf. They stuck out, just a little bit above the skin.I could see it through the holes they made in my shirt. I flexed my wings back again. They were about as long as my arm span, if not a little longer. Paper thin by the glances I was getting.

The veins were black just like my veins were now. I didn't think that was going to go away. But I could live with that. You could see through my wings, they were slightly tinted red. Probably from my flames. At the very tip of my wings were little black horns. Didn't need to be a reaper to get mine, I guess. I think they were very fitting. I spread my arms and wings out, bringing them in an arch to cocoon myself.

Some reapers started to inch towards me. Shooting their gazes between me and Death, not entirely sure what she would want them to do.

Stumbling back, I raised a hand, "Stay back," Fire once again lurched forward. I held my hand as if I was the one who got burned.

The fire landed in front of them but they still stumbled back.

"I'm sorry, I'm sorry." I turned to look at Death. At Rylan.

Falling to my knees, I cupped my hands to my chest, afraid to reach out to anyone. Luckily, I didn't have to. Rylan came, he let himself drop in front of me. My flames died down enough for him to take my hands in his.

"Hi." I said it softly. Not wanting to provoke anything from anyone or myself.

"Look at me, Rhyd." I didn't want to.

He placed a tentative hand on my cheek and gently pushed my face up so I would have to either look or fight him. I looked.

I was worried he would be afraid. Or even worse, disgusted. But that's not what I saw. All I saw was love.

"You are beautiful."

I choked on my next breath. I leaned into him, careful to extinguish myself. The only flames that remained were on my wings and I wrapped those around us both. This was a private moment.

"I didn't want this. I never wanted this."I cried.

"I know, baby, I know." He held onto me, "But hey, you are stronger than this. You are strong and beautiful and can kick my ass from here to Timbuktu."

He knew just how to make me laugh. Which I did. I looked up at him. "Thank you." I put a hand on one cheek and gently kissed the other. " For everything."

Unraveling my wings, we both stood up. He walked a little ways away from me as I came face to face with Death. I shook my head at her. And walked away.

That led me to Allison, she looked a little terrified but not of me, I think. At the situation, I hope. I placed a hand on her shoulder and she leaned into it.

"Don't worry about me, okay? Keep yourself safe." She just nodded, tears in her eyes. I truly hoped that she was not horrified by me. I know we were raised hunters but neither of us are human anymore.

Next up was Clark. I narrowed my gaze, the flames coming back up a bit. He had the decency to take a step back. It made me smile. Maybe it was my smugness or he just caught himself but he squared his jaw and took that step forward again.

"And, you," I paused for maximum effect, letting him get a good feel of the flames

I could call up, "Protect her, or I'm going to be barbecuing you for dinner." I almost laughed when he looked horrified but I sent a wink to Allison and she had to hide her giggle.

Turning back to Death, I looked her up and down. I didn't need to say anything. I let her in so she could see whatever she wanted to. All the panic and adoration and pain and what I've come to realize what might just be love. She gave a slight smile and all I did was give a nod in return.

I walked over to the reapers who were bravely waiting for me. "Come on, boys. I think there's somewhere you were wanting to take me." I walked beside them. No more fighting. Not that any of them would dare touch me after what they just witnessed. I let them lead me back towards camp. One grabbed me and we sped up so we could actually make it to the camp. I saw Rylan speed up behind me, he grabbed the hand of the reaper that was guarding my back. Looks like he was coming with me. I wasn't worried. I knew this was for the best.

"You should go with Death. You need to be helping with the case while I'm away." I said it like I was going on vacation and not a jail cell. I just kept telling myself that this was for the best. The more I said it, the more I could believe it. The more I believed it, the less he had to worry.

Death would keep me updated. There's nothing in this case that I wouldn't know about. I've been studying it ever since I got here. They needed my help. But I'll hurt people. I understood that. I know what I'm becoming. And it scared the hell out of me.

7 ROUND TWO

They took me into a room off of the war room. It was encased in a plexiglass. I recognized it immediately. It was fireproof. I tried not to be hurt with the thought that they have been planning this for a while. Death must have known or seen something in me. She knew she'd have to put me in here.

I screamed and Rylan popped up on the other side of my glass. It was like I was in an interrogation room. I've been in a few. I should know. Except this time all the cops are scared to come in with me. I stopped screaming. I was just trying to figure out if it was sound proof or not.

I walked over and put a hand on the glass, just like any other cheesy, lame chick-flick. He placed his over the shadow of mine. "Go help Death."

He shook his head. "I'm not leaving you alone."

"Yes, you are. I'm fine in here. I can see all the information we have on the boards, I can talk to you guys. I'm fine here."

I backed away from the glass and looked around me. There was a table in the corner full of food and a coffee maker and I noticed that someone had placed some books on the shelf above it. I went over to see what they were. They were from Death's room, I recognized them. She brought in the one that I kept looking at, even if I never began reading it, it drew my attention and I'd just sit there staring at it for hours. I rubbed the book like it was an old friend. I held it to my chest as I looked around the rest of my box. There was a metal table in the center, it looked like it was screwed into the floor. There was a metal wheely chair in front of it. I sat down in it. Putting the book on the table, I spun around like a child. Or a bored teenager in high school.

"What if I need to pee?"Rylanpointed off to the left. I looked and noticed a door for the first time. Under further inspection it led to the bathroom that had always been in the war room. I snorted.

"What if you need to pee?"

He pointed out the window towards the woods. I laughed but it quickly died out.

I looked at Rylan but I noticed something shiny on my childish spin around my enclosed little world. I stopped and looked above my speaking glass. There was a round metal opening in the wall. I glanced around again and noticed that there were several more strategically placed around the room. I had a feeling I knew what they were.

"Please, tell me those aren't for water?"

Rylan didn't try to deny it. He looked away, guilty. I guess that answered that.

"Great." I went up and stood on my tiptoes to reach it. They were freezing. That wasn't going to be hot water. So I couldn't even lose it in here without getting myself hurt. Fabulous. "You better hope no one tries to drown me in here." I meant it as a joke but he didn't smile.

I sighed. "You need to go," I told Rylan. I went back to my flat foot. I wanted to see just how well these little sprinklers worked. Not everything I do involves fire. I smirked.

I rubbed my hands together. I knew he was protected by the glass but I didn't want him to be here. He needed to be where he would be most useful. And that was at the most recent crime scene. I kept rubbing my hands together, blew into them and a little spark began. I looked up at the nozzles. Nothing was happening.

I pulled them apart and rubbed my fingers together, watching as a tiny wave began. I could feel them heating up. The fire was slowly reaching my eyes. I was getting better at controlling it in such a short time. My veins were still black. I guess I had no choice but to live with it.

Soon enough there was fire coming from my hands but that's not what I wanted. I focused them just to the inside of my hands. I pulsed them closer and farther apart. Trying to get to what I wanted. I saw little flickers of blue but it wasn't big enough.

I slapped my hands together and there was a loud crash. The chair I was sitting on toppled over, smoke coming from it. One of the nozzles started spilling out water. It wasn't like a pump where it would just fall into the room. It was on where it sprayed you no matter where you were. It aimed itself at the chair but I'm sure it was coming for me next. I slapped my hands together once more and blue lightning was strung in between my fingers.

I aimed my hands at two different nozzles. I snapped my fingers. Lightning went out. I could hear it sizzling with the spouts. I could hear the metal trying not to give under my supernatural power. But I was a freak of nature and metal was man-made. The two nozzles made a popping sound and then there was smoke filling the room. So it's not fire that they don't like, it's smoke. That's what triggers them to come on.

I looked back at Rylan and he was gone. Finally listened to me, for once. I hoped he actually went to be productive and not just to go tell Death that I was breaking her new toys. I went to the very far corner and just sat there. Twirling the fire between my fingers. I made a little snake and it slithered up and down my arm. Tracing my entire body and not burning a single part of me. It was rather beautiful, if I do say so myself. Sad that I had to make my own friend, though.

This was going to suck. I had nothing to do and I had no way to help unless they came back with information. Who knew how often they would come to update me? I am a very forgettable person.

I just kept playing with my fire. That's when I heard the clapping. I turned to see Clark emerge from the shadows. I had no idea how long he was standing there.

"What a show, Rhydian. Very impressive with your little magic trick." I don't know why but my wings flicked out.

He just irked me. "Shouldn't you be out there investigating while I'm in here?"

"Oh, I just had to see it. This famous hunter losing her grind. Losing her pride. Just sitting there. One hundred and fifty pound ball of rage. Locked in a box."

I narrowed my eyes and stood up, it didn't even bother me that he mentioned my weight, incorrectly, of course. What kind of man would speak to a woman in such a way? "What the hell is your problem?"

He stepped very close to the glass. "You are my problem. And I could make it go away with just the press of a button." he flicked his eyes over to where his hand rested on a bright blue button. I hadn't noticed it before. I knew what that button would do. I may not have noticed it in my initial scope of the room, but it's purpose was blatantly obvious. I shook my head.

"They would just think you set them off yourself. It wouldn't be all that surprising." He pressed it. Water started pouring out of all the spouts left. There were at least six of them. I looked around, panicked.

"What did I ever do to you?" He responded but I couldn't hear him with the sound of water surrounding me. It was already up to my ankles. This entire room was fireproof. It would hold water inside. With me. Clark just walked away. He left me there.

What the hell is going on?

I sat on the table and the water followed me, forcing me off. I was shoved under the water. I inhaled on accident. I came up coughing. Looking around, I couldn't find anything that I could use to stop the water. It was already at my waist. There was no way that I could start a fire in here. Not while I was being pelted with freezing water. I stood back up on the table. The water didn't stop and it kept coming.

I looked in the bathroom from my perch, at the bookcase, all around. There was nothing in here that would help me break the glass. It was to my chest.

I was panicking, wading back and forth on the table, searching and trying to stay warm. I tried to scream but water would just go straight down my throat. All of a sudden, I saw Death. I was now underwater. I stood on my tiptoes on the table to try to catch some air. Once again, I got pushed off.

The entire room was full and I had no idea how long I could hold my breath. She must've sensed my death coming. She came to collect.

Then I opened my eyes and felt a giant pull take me with it. I was rushed out of the room with the water because someone opened the door. I hit the farthest wall with a thump. Death loomed over me. I sucked in air like it was from the fountain of youth.

"Why did you set them off?"

"Why'd you put a goddamn panic button in there?" I said it around my coughing. Looks like I could hold my breath for longer than I thought.

"Someone hit the button." I closed my mind off right there. No one needed to know that Clark just tried to kill me. I wanted to figure out that one on my own. No one else needs to be distracted from the real case. There's any number of petty reasons why he would want to kill me. Just like there are plenty for me wanting to kill him. I just nodded.

"Yeah, I think Rylan accidently hit it on his way out. Dumbass. Stupid of you to put that kind of fucking button there anyway." I tried to sound neutral but I don't know how well it worked. She looked like she wanted to argue and press the issue but I kept my mind shut up even tighter. Locking that door. I got better at hiding from her. And I wasn't sure if that was really a good thing or not.

She changed the subject. "You weren't even in there for two hours and I already have to take you out."

"Well," I winked," I was always safest with you in the first place." That made Death laugh and it made me smile. Anything to hide the truth.

I remember what Clark said now. When I asked him what I did to him. He said I took everything from him. I guess he wants to take everything from me, too. I had to get to him. I sobered immediately. A new panic filling me.

"Allison!" I had to get to her!

Death looked very confused. "I have to go. Right now. Where is she?"

"Oh, she went to the library with Clark to speak with Martin." I let my wings come out and shook them off, every minute they changed a little more. They had begun to grow dark brown feathers. It seems some parts evolve faster than others.

I flew out of there as fast as I could make myself. I hit the wall and knocked into the door frame. I was a new flyer and running probably would have been faster but I didn't have time to be stopped by anyone. The wind through my brand new feathers was a feeling I could never explain to anyone. It was amazing, and even that didn't give it the credit they deserve. But I didn't have time to revel in that. I had to find my sister.

I kept trying to fly as fast as they would take me but I kept hitting branches or running into entire trees. Eventually I gave up and fell to the ground. I twisted my ankle on the way down. I cursed. I began to run as fast as my tired body could go. I had to make it to my sister. I weaved around trees and jumped over bushes. My ankle was throbbing, I think it might be broken but that was not going to stop me. I could see the end of the cliff and I knew I didn't have time to take the stairs. I didn't think I could make it to the stairs to begin with. I could feel my veins pulsing towards my leg. Trying to mend itself. I never had that power before but I did know that some witches had it. Looks like I was one of them now.

I pushed myself until I reached the end of the cliff. And I jumped. Arms extended like someone jumping off a high dive, I let my wings back out. I soared down and landed on the ledge. The door was open. I slid in as quietly as possible. Thank god, they cooperated enough for that, otherwise I would be at the bottom of that cliff.

I didn't hear anything which was pretty impressive with my hearing. I limped in. There were wood chips everywhere. I had no idea what they were from. Considering the damage to the shelves and tables, which they were from would be more accurate.

"Martin? I need your help." I searched for him in the rafters, creeping forward. I headed over towards the nook that we shared our first conversation in. It probably wasn't smart to be talking but if Clark was still in here then he would already know that I was inside.

I turned the corner and felt a sharp pain in my chest. I wanted to cry. There was a path of wood pieces that I followed back there. And now I knew what they were from. There was a large pile of the chippings in front of the nook. And I found Martin. He was scattered all about the first floor. And his head sat right where I did when we first met. I fell to my knees in front of him.

I took Martin and pressed him to my chest. That's when the vision started. I sucked in a breath like I was about to go underwater. I could see Clark and Allison. Clark had her pressed against him with a hand over her mouth. They walked, awkwardly, in and Martin flew over.

"How may I assist y.. Unhand her at once, young man!" That was all he got to say. Martin flew over and tried to peck at Clark's hands. Clark flung Allison to the floor. She hit her head against the stairs. I saw her trying to get up. Clark pulled out a gun, it looked remarkably like mine that had only hours ago been confiscated, and he just kept firing at Martin. In his untrained hands, bullets flew out. Martin was able to dodge those first few but soon enough, he got hit. Martin was down and Clark kept firing until there was nothing left of him, until the clip was emptied. All of Martin was destroyed, except for his head. I would cry for him. Later, I would. I only got to see him once. I never got the chance to tell him my story.

I followed as Clark picked him up and started to whisper something to him. I couldn't understand the words. It took me only a moment before I knew what he was doing. He wanted me to see this. I watched as Clark brought him over to our nook and set him down on the cushions. He kissed his head and apologized. I saw him squat down so Martin's eyes were looking right at him. Through him.

"I hope you enjoyed the show." And Clark walked away. I could hear Allison scream when he reached her. And then it was gone.

"I thought you'd want to see what happened to your friend." I turned and grabbed a knife from one of my leg straps, Death knew they were there but didn't let the reapers take them from me. I never took them off.

Allison was held against his chest like in the little playback. Only now there were several gashes along her face and body. I can only say that because now she was naked. She wasn't in the vision and I can only imagine what he's done to her while they've been waiting for me. I could've broken down right there for her. I closed my eyes for a second when I noticed the blood going down her leg. When my eyes opened again, they burned.

"Let her go. She doesn't have anything to do with this, Clark. It's me you want." I had my hands out because I noticed where the gun was. He has it pressed against her temple.

He laughed. It was strange, it didn't sound quite like him. Like when someone calls you by the wrong name and you try to just brush it off. "She's not going anywhere."

I crinkle my eyebrows together. "We've met each other before, haven't we? Before you died, or maybe while you were a reaper, I don't know but we know each other, yeah?"

That could be the only reason that he was doing this to me. Attacking my sister, trying to have me killed, killing Martin. It was all for me. I did something to him and he wanted payback. This plan of his was a long time in the making.

I clenched my fists. Fire was my friend. I could feel it building up inside me, and that was something he could not take away. I flung my knife at Clark, aiming for his head but I missed my mark and hit his hand. He cursed and dropped Allison. Wasn't what I was going for but I'd take it.

I slid over and grabbed her. Kicking up so I would be pushing Clark away. I put her in the nook with Martin. I crouched down because I couldn't see Clark anymore. I couldn't hear him either. He must be cloaking himself or something to be able to hide from me.Glamour, that's what they called it.

"Why's he doin this?" I put my hand back behind me and grabbed her leg so she knew I was there for her, still looking for him. She flinched.

"Shh. I don't know, darlin. I don't know." I crawled forward and peeked around the corner. I kept crawling and looked up the stairs.

I felt him before I saw him. I tried to scramble away but Clark was already behind me. He grabbed me by my hair and yanked downward to knock me off my feet.

"How does it feel knowing that you can't protect her from me? How does it feel knowing that I can play with her whenever I want whether she likes it or not? How does it make you feel knowing I can take everything from you?"

My hands were above my head, clasping onto his wrist. All that fire building up, I made sure it went straight to my hands. He cried out and backed away only to come right back and slam me against the floor. He managed to pick me up with his uninjured hand and throw me through the banister on the second floor.

I hit the bookshelf and I watched as it toppled on top of me. Well, it would have. I pushed out with my hands and curled up. A circular, me sized hole was in the bookshelf. Just big enough for me. I stood up. I noticed that my ankle didn't hurt anymore. I looked around for Clark. I knew I wouldn't be able to see him so I focused on my other senses. The hair on the back of my neck raised.

I lifted my arm and turned around quick enough to block his swing and land one in his gut, again and again and again. I did it until I backed him into a wall. My hands were still coated in flames as was my hair. I pushed him against the wall and threw him into a corner.

He could never take everything from me. In my fiery haze, I didn't pay attention to the floor. I tripped. That gave him enough time to get up and shove me back to where I just had him.

His body was perfectly against mine and my face shoved into drywall. One of his hands held both of my wrists above my head. He was careful enough to avoid my hands. His other hand roughly grazed the side of my body.

"Hell, I don't know why I bother faking it with your sister. I could've been with you this entire time." He made it up to my chest, harshly grabbing my breast.

"She loved you!" I spread the fire down my arms and up my body, forcing him to drop me or get burnt.

Clark backed up a bit too far and fell off the second floor, considering there wasn't a banister there anymore. I didn't hear a thump so I rushed over and didn't see him on the ground.

"Allison!" I jumped. My wings softened the landing. No need to be impaired again. And I was getting better at using them.

I came around the corner to find him holding Allison. She was on his lap like a child. And she looked terrified.

"You know, this all would've been easier if you would just die already. You could've stopped all of this. You could've died with that witch or that werewolf pack, or your boyfriend could've done it, or back when I tried to drown you. This all could've been avoided. But no," he licked the side of Allison's face, she whimpered, "You just refuse to die."

"Kill me now. Hell, I'll let you. Just let her go." I was confused by what he said, I remember all of those instances well. Things I blamed myself for, where people I loved had gotten hurt.

He laughed. "No, it's too late for that." He kissed one of her temples and leaned in close to her ear. I couldn't catch what he was saying.

Tears rolled down Allison's face. "Please, don't do this, baby."

He lifted his head up to make eye contact with me. I shook my head. And he snapped her neck. "No!" He vanished. I didn't bother looking for his glamour, I knew he wasn't here anymore. I rushed over and picked up Allison. Everything seemed to slow down as she lay there, limp in my arms.

"No,no,no! Come on, Ally. Come on, please! No! Help us!" I knew no one could hear us but I kept screaming anyway. I doubt it was from my yelling but Death did appear then. I was engulfing myself in flames. Allison's body was already beginning to disappear. I started to cry and it felt like ashes blowing across my face. My sister, once again, laid dead in my arms. And this time, she wasn't coming back. I couldn't do anything to stop it. My poor baby sister had to go through all this suffering because of me. Her only crime was being related to me.

"No, no, no! Come on, Ally. Not again, you can't do this again, please." I rocked with what was left of her for a while. My fire drying my tears.

I picked her up, she would be completely gone by the time I got back to the camp but I didn't care. I wasn't leaving her alone, not this time. Not here.

"Where is he?" All the anger, and sorrow, and pain came out bundled into one emotion. Rage.

"I do not know. He has found a way to cloak himself from me."

"Then uncloak him!" I just kept looking at my dead sister. The tears had already stopped. Death just kind of lingered, saddened.

I shoved her against a wall, even with my sister's ash still in my arms, "Tell me where he is." I spoke slowly and gritted the words out.

"She is right, you know?"

"Martin?" I spun around to see if it was really him. And there he was, whole again. Sitting where he once lied dead.

"He comes back to life in my presence. That has always been the case. This is no different."

"Well, lucky him." I couldn't even be happy that my new friend was not permanently dead.

"She does not know where he is and unfortunately, I do not either. But you cannot give up."

"He's been doing all of this. Something was off about him, why don't you go figure out what?" Allison was gone. I headed toward the door.

"What are you going to do?" Death kept appearing in front of me, only to disappear when I would've walked into her. At one point, I was too close and I walked through her. I didn't know she could do that and I did not stop to think about it.

I doused my flames. "I'm gonna find that son of a bitch."

"And then what?" Martin landed on a ledge near the door. That's who spoke.

Hearing his voice made me feel better. It didn't stop the rage filling me but knowing that at least one person I cared about wasn't dead meant the world to me.

"Kill him." I flew out the door. I didn't let either of them stop me. I could feel Death flying behind me but eventually she went back to the ledge and I felt her eyes follow me everywhere I went. I let her, nothing phased me.

I knew he wouldn't be anywhere I would look for him. I jumped off the ledge and flew around the entire cliff side anyway. It was a giant canyon, I guess I never realized that in the rush of crime scenes. There were many little crevices and dips in the walls. I stopped and looked in every last one of them. By the time I got back to the cliff side, it was dark. The fire returned to my arms and hair. I don't know if it was a reaction to the darkness or my emotions ringing at their peak.

I could hear screeching from the air above me. I landed next to Death and searched for what that sound could be coming from.

"They're coming." I looked at Death, she searched the sky.

"Jesus Christ, what now!?" It was more of an enraged statement than a question. She answered me anyway.

She leaned her head towards me, still seeking the monsters that are coming. "The seven have been taken and accepted. The doors have been opened. It's Armageddon."

I closed my eyes. I could hear the bones of wings flapping. It was ripping through the air.

"Do you hear that?" I turned around. There was something running towards us from the forest. The screech came again. Death and I went back to back. I was still facing the forest.

"We need higher ground." I flew up to the top of the cliff. Death floated, still against my back. I could hear whatever was coming and it was coming soon.

"Do you know what they are?"

"There's a griffin coming from above and a cretan bull headed in your direction." I didn't actually expect an answer but the more you know, right? I took in a deep breath, I could smell them both but that didn't give me any more information than what Death did.

"Great. Know how to kill 'em?"

"Not a clue."

"Great." That's when my battle buddy came stomping through to the clearing. "Holy shi.." And it charged. I lunged to the right and hoped Death moved out of the way.

My veins were pumping hard, already prepared to heal any injury. It was in great contrast to the white bull that quickly turned around to charge me again. It was the most beautiful creature I've ever seen. It was all white with gold feather like attachments on its shoulders and hind quarters. It's tail was much longer than it should have been and based on the way it was throwing it at me, I was sure it was a lot harder, too.

I jumped over it's swinging tail and landed on my stomach. I rolled over so I was under it and reached up to touch it, my hands engulfed in flames. I could see lightning flicker from my fingers. I had to quickly roll away because it tried to trample me instead of run like I was hoping it would.

I pulled knives out of every pocket and holster I had. I could fling them left and right, trying to hit some form of soft surface that would kill it. At least wound it. I flung one at its head. It landed in it's bullseye, no pun intended. But that is what I was aiming for. It backed up and tried to shake it out. That was my time to strike but I turned to make sure Death was still alive. I couldn't hear her.

It was the most silent fight I have ever seen. I forgot that a griffin was mostly a giant cat. It stalked around Death and I only had one blade left. I looked at it and back at my own opponent. I closed my eyes and threw. It landed in the back of the neck of the griffin. Not what I was aiming for but it was enough to distract it. Death flew down and placed both her hands on the griffin's lion head. I could see her veins pop with the focus she was using. It fell to its knees. Which was a far drop considering that they were both flying.

That's when the bull rammed into me. It's horns didn't pierce me like I thought it was hoping for. It shoved me back. I grabbed onto it's horns and dug my feet into the ground. It took longer than I liked but I was able to stop our tug-of-war. It was close, too. He almost ran me off of the cliff. Not that that was a major concern anymore.

I pushed the flames to grow hotter on my hands. The Cretan whined and I pushed harder. Moving my hands and my body. I engulfed it's horns and I shoved my body back, away from the edge.

It was like walking through quicksand. It was slow and painful but I got us away and kept shoving. I gave one last push and twisted myself so I was on its back. And it took me back to when my father would take Allison and I to rodeos when we were young. It was a goal of mine to learn what the bull riders did. And I learned it well.

Unlike a bull rider, I wrapped my legs around its neck instead of it's core and held on for dear life. I tightened them as hard as I possibly could and I kept them there. Following Death's example, I placed both of my hands on the Cretan's head. And I let it all out. All the pain, and anger, and anguish. I let it all flow to my hands. I could feel my veins being pumped with black magic and darkness but I didn't care. I felt the fire inside me and I let it out. Someone had to pay for this and right now it was this damn bull who thought he could come here and take what was mine.

"Time to play." I laughed but soon I was screaming with rage and all the pain and energy it took to focus that much fire in one place. The bull's head was completely engulfed in flames and I rubbed my hands against its charring furr. Blue lightning traced its way around and around its body.

I jumped off to watch my destruction, landing on one knee. The bull wasn't quite done fighting and he kicked the dirt preparing to charge. I let him come. And when he got close, I inched my fingers together and thrusted my arm up and out when I was underneath him.

I didn't turn around but he kept running and then I heard a heavy thud. I looked down at my hand, the bull's hearting giving its last beat.

I wasn't finished. I walked over to the bull's body and closed my eyes. Slowly I pushed my fingers into its skull. Not like I was breaking into it but like it was water and I was becoming a part of it. I sunk in like when I walked through Death. And I let it rip. I released it. I don't care what you are, there's no coming back from that. Hooray, hooray, the Cretan bull is dead. It still lifted its head, I don't know how. I rolled off since I was on its head so my legs wouldn't get caught underneath it. When in doubt, tuck and roll. It's head fell to the ground and it never moved again.

I landed once again with one knee on the ground and one hand. My head was down but I flung it up when I heard a crashing sound, hair flying everywhere. I stood and almost fell. I laughed and looked down at myself. There was a giant gash on my side that I don't remember getting. The heat of the battle must have distracted me too much. I raised my eyes to see what was going on.

I watched as Death used my very small throwing dagger to finish cutting off the head of the griffin. She dropped it and the knife. We were the winners. I wondered who would win between us. I was game to find out. I bit my lip and smiled. Death looked up at me then.

"No." There was so much power echoing through her voice that it froze me in place. She walked over to me and I couldn't move. We were both covered in blood. She tucked all the hair behind my ears and lifted my chin.

"All that fire, locked in a box." It was too close to what Clark said when he tried to kill me. Flames crawled back up my arms. I still couldn't move. But the flames kept growing.

"Uh, uh, ah." She shook her head. "Not this time." And she pulled me into her. She had me by the back of the neck and kissed me so roughly I couldn't help but smile. My head jerked to one side and I tried to push her away.

"D," I managed to mumble across her lips.

"I'm," kiss.

"Fine," kiss.

"Now," kiss.

"I am not." She kept kissing me. I tried to back away but she followed me. Until we hit a tree. I tried to push her away again but she grabbed my hands and placed them above my head, I groaned.

"No, stop." I turned my head so she was no longer kissing me. She continued her trek to my neck. My eyes rolled back. She shook her head.

"Death, I said stop." I shoved against her. She didn't stop. She kept going lower and lower.

"Stop!" My entire body was a fireball, she did stop then. She backed up with a hustle. I saw it then. A little shimmering glow above her head. I reached out for it and it singed away. I didn't even have to touch it.

Death stumbled. "What happened?"

I rolled my eyes, even though I was no longer mad at her. It wasn't her fault, after all. Even though I'm not sure who's fault it was exactly but I had a pretty good guess. "You were getting frisky."

She looked confused and then understanding dawned on her. "Rhydian, I am so sorry. You know I would never.."

I put a fiery hand up. "I know."

I stopped making flames. "How did this happen?" Oh, she was pissed now.

“Clark, happened. I had no idea you reapers had so much magic.”

“They don’t. I suppose he could be tapping into mine.”

“They can do that?” I sat down on a boulder near the edge of the cliff. I just realized now that that bull could have pushed me over the edge and I would’ve been fine. I ruffled my feathers. It would have died faster than me. It did die faster than me.

“Only the few who I let.”

“How many did you let in?” This would have been great information to know days ago. That reminds me of how little sleep I’ve gotten. Hardly any since that first night. I counted back. I’ve been here for over a month. I rubbed my face.

“Two.”

“And let me guess, one is dead and one is rogue.”

“Yes. But they can only tap into my power if they know how and that I did not teach them so that means that Clark is receiving outside help, possibly from a witch. But it is very dangerous for them to use this level of power. It changes you, it would turn a reaper into someone else. He might not even realize what he’s doing.”

"Peachy. So glad I figured out why he seemed off. You're telling me it's as if Clark has multiple personalities? Is that what we're going with? " I stood and started walking towards the camp. Death sucked in a breath.

I looked back at her. "What?"

"We have to get back. Now!" She grabbed me and we disappeared. We appeared again, already in the camp.

"Oh, my god." There was a fire everywhere. It pulled me in. Called to me. I wanted to be a part of it. Death was more concerned with something else.

There was a pile of dead reapers in the center of the fighting pit. I could see that shimmer that was over Death.

"They killed each other." We stumbled forward. Stopping at the edge of the ring.

"How do you know?" Her voice sounded hollow, cold. Like she would never know happiness again. Maybe she wouldn't.

"You don't see the magic floating above them?"

She shook her head. I noticed in the front of the fighting pit was her goat, as well.

"You have to stop the blaze."

I looked at her like she was crazy. "I create fire. I can't take it back."

"Yes, my love, you can. You just have to want it. Accept it, let the fire back inside you."

I didn't believe a word she just said. "Just accept it, alright, easy enough. Um, that is not my fire, that's going to burn me alive." I mumbled under my breath.

"No, it will not."

She said it so matter-of-factly that it was hard to argue with her. But it was my life and body she expects to hop in there. Doing this in reverse was going to hurt, if it was even possible.

I focused as hard as I possibly could, tapping into what was calling me to it. I inhaled and nothing happened.

"Keep trying."

I rolled my eyes. Demanding, this one. I closed my eyes. I searched for the flames in my senses, I felt it as if it moved with me. Walking forward, I felt the flames become a part of me, unburning. I sucked in all the air around me.

I moved my arms from one direction to the other, spinning and rotating with it. Creating a funnel of flames with me at its center. I pulled all of the flames in instead of spreading it out.

A shout escaped my lips and I fell to my knees. I wasn't done yet. Too much heat that wasn't from me. It wasn't burning me so much as boiling me from the inside. I had to put a hand on the ground and I keeled over. I kept bringing it in. I could feel the tears rolling down my face and another scream escaped me but I didn't stop. I took one last deep breath and it was gone. The flames were gone.

And when I was done, I collapsed. I opened my eyes without realizing that they had still been closed. On the ground, I pointed a single finger at the pile of disappearing, decomposing bodies. And I let it all back out. One last pyre. No one else was going to die here.

"I can hear them. The rest are in the war room. Go." Death disappeared again. When she came back, the last of the remaining reapers followed.

Death came over and picked me up. She looked upon all of her children. What was left of them, I saw Rylan in the crowd as well. "Tonight, we have suffered a great loss. Get some sleep. Come tomorrow, we will be preparing for battle." She walked away, still carrying me. She took me back to her cabin and softly placed me on the bed.

“Get some sleep, sugar. You are going to need it.”

8 PERSPECTIVE

I opened my eyes. I didn't move. Death was sitting on the edge of the bed, reading. Her back was to me so I couldn't be sure. It seemed like who she was as a person. Well, not a person per say. I sat up on my elbow to watch her.

"You were having another nightmare." She continued to read, I heard her turn a page. I had a feeling she was just skimming through it like her entire essence was surrounding me.

"Well, that's nothing new to me."

"This one is new, though, my dear." She's been in my head again. It didn't really bother me. I knew if she would have asked, I would have told her. Everything. There's no point in trying to hide it, she would just find out.

"D, my sister just died. Again. What did you expect? Rainbows and butterflies and ice cream? Not rape scenes, getting beat, literally everything that happened to my sister? I'm never going to be able to unsee him wrapping his hands around her throat and twisting.

Tossing her away like she meant nothing. Like she was trash."

Tears ran down my face, I didn't try to hide them. I closed my eyes only to see my sister lying there, unmoving. "I can make you forget." I could feel Death reach a hand out towards me. I caught it.

"Don't even think that. I have to remember. I need this anger. I need this pain to fuel me for what I need to do. I need to remember. Somebody has to remember who she was. Before and after. And I'm the only one left to do that for her."

I dropped her hand like it was hot, even though I was the one with heat and she was stone cold. She placed her hand on my cheek. I turned my face into it, resting against it. "Whatever you desire, my love."

"Why's he doing this to us?" I held back my tears this time. There would be time for that later. But for today, for now, I had to focus. For me. For all the dead. Or Death. For my sister.

"From the beginning, I had thought that it was all about me. It is evident now that it is for you. All that he is doing, he is doing it for you. We must figure out why because I certainly do not know."

"Maybe I killed someone he loved before he died. That's the only thing I can think of because I don't recognize him."

Death hugged me to her and began to pet my hair. I hid my face in her neck. I could feel the scars against my skin from where I bit her. I was surprised she even had scars. I saw her heal.

"I let the scar appear. I heal just as I normally would but I leave the effect there. I like to see how the world has marked me. Since after all, we all began as a blank canvas."

"The world didn't do that to you. I did."

"And you are a part of this world. And a part of mine." I cuddled back into her neck. I did that to her and she practically thanked me for it.

I held her for I don't know how long. Or, I guess, she was holding me. Either way, neither of us were letting go. Contact seemed to help. It helped me deal with the fact that I wouldn't be touching my sister again or my father or any of my friends.

"Everyone keeps dying on me."

"I'm still here." I turned around to see Rylan standing in the doorway. Which was funny because Death spoke the same thing at the same time. It made me smile.

I got up and hugged him, practically jumping into his arms. "I thought you were with the rest of the dead."

He hugged me back, pulling away slightly to look into my eyes. "You can't get rid of me that easily." He looked as if he wanted to kiss me, glancing down at my lips every once in a while.

I stepped away from him and turned so I could look at them both. "Yes, I still have both of you but for how long? Eventually, I'll die and I won't have you anymore. And you," I looked over to my long lost lover, my shield, my best friend, "And eventually, one of us will die. It comes with our line of work. I'm sure there were times that we were supposed to die but we can't escape it forever."

I knew he was thinking about the same thing as me. The first time we met. When he should've killed me and I wanted to kill him. I wish he would have. Everyday I wish I could take it back and have him kill me. I don't want to be like this. I try not to act the way I do but when the fire starts I can't control it. It's a draw that feels far too good to even think about pulling away from.

"That is something that we can all help you with." That was Death.

"Death!"

We all rushed out the door toward the shouting and leaned over the ledge. There were reapers lined up, only five of them. There were only about fifteen of them left.

"It's ready."

I looked farther down and all the other reapers were in a circle. In the fighting pit. "What's going on?" I looked between Death, suspicious.

"It's time to help control yourself." Rylan's voice came from behind me. I looked over my shoulder at him and he shoved me. I fell over the railing but caught a hold of the ledge. I looked up at both of them, betrayal filling me. Rylan looked sad, stepping on my fingers to force me to let go. I did. I landed on my feet. Hell, call me Cat now.

"What the hell?" The reapers that were lined up all grabbed me, none too gently either. "Get your hands off me!" They didn't, they dragged me over to the fighting pit. And now I knew what they were doing. The fire had already begun to build. I could already feel it in my eyes. They were trying to piss me off.

"No, you don't know what you're doing. Please." They threw me in the middle of them all. A kick came from nowhere and made me fall to a knee. I saw a girl walk over and she traced a finger over my face. I recognized her as Mave. She punched downward and I fell face first in the dirt. I coughed. Fire had started on the inside.

"You don't know what you're about to start." I could feel my gums shifting. It hurt. Like hell. I opened my mouth and felt my teeth. They felt fine but I think I knew they wouldn't feel the same in a few seconds. I was evolving again. I got up.

"I said back off!" I knew I didn't actually say that but it was implied and they do not want to be near me when I begin to shift again. Whatever that might be into. That's when I saw him. He was on the outskirts of the circle. Walking slowly, deliberately letting me see him. I stood there a second to make sure I wasn't hallucinating. Then I burst into flames. It seemed out of place and out of the blue but that was all it took for me.

"You should not have come back here." I rolled my head across my shoulders. Loving the cracks that came with it. This was going to be fun. I looked at Death. "Is it time to play now?" She nodded.

I didn't know why I asked for permission but it was like a small box full of a monsterous heat. And Death had the key. I think I liked this better. It was like having a leash. And master just let me off of it.

I let the fire emerge from my hands. I walked over to Clark. "Come on, big boy. I'm bored." I let loose. I made a circle around us. No one was going to stop me from killing him. Not this time. It was time to end this.

He lunged for me. I dodged and brought my elbow down on the back of his neck. Not hard enough. I frowned. He fell forward and turned back to me. He threw a fist. Left, right, left, left, left, right. I knew this style. It wasn't Clark's. I didn't care. He tried to lunge for me again and I grabbed him by the neck.

"I don't think your game is working, D. Can I just kill him now?" I was going to do it either way. There was a fire burning his throat as well as my hand tightening. I lifted his feet off of the ground. And he wavered. There was a shimmer in the air around him and soon I was no longer looking at Clark. I was slowly killing my best friend.

I snarled and flung him to the ground. My fangs finally came through my gums. Now I just wanted to sink them into something. Into someone.

"Where is he?" It was more of a screaming demand than a question.

I was looking at Death but I turned my glare to Rylan. I stalked back over to him. I grabbed him by the shirt and shook him. "WHERE IS HE?!"

Rylan shook his head, not really afraid, just concerned. I snarled at him again. I opened my mouth to end this useless carcass. Then I couldn't breath. I started to choke. I looked down and dropped Rylan. He fell to the ground. I started to cough until I too fell to the ground. I glanced up at Death. She held up a glowing key. I was panicked, I touched my throat. And there it was. There was a collar on me. I could feel it. It was made of energy. I wondered if my energy was stronger. It was just a metaphor, after all. I didn't think Death would take me seriously.

"Man, I think there's a show about this. Got your little monster on a leash, huh? Gonna make me do your bidding, D?"

"Of course not, Rhydian. It will let you do whatever you want. Except hurt innocents. Figure out what they have done to you then you can do what you want to them."

"What if they're just annoying me?" I crouched down and tilted my head.

"Nice try, love. It will not be on there for long, I assure you. I will let you 'loose' when we track down where Clark is hiding out. And it will only appear when the fire appears."

Good thing fire isn't my only weapon now. I licked my fangs at her.

"Were you actually going to kill me?" Rylan stood up.

"Is this one of those times when you want me to lie to protect your delicate feelings?"

He made eye contact with Death. I looked between them. She nodded. I backed away as he approached. I kept backing up until I felt hands on my back. I lit my back up and immediately started choking until I doused it but they still backed up. I only knew because I was able to keep moving in reverse. I started coughing again when the flames snaked around my fingers. Freaking collar. I'm not a dog. Eventually, I hit a wall. My head lifted up with the impact and my mouth opened. Which brought my head right into his hands. He put one on each side of my head. My mouth was still open so he slid his mouth right against mine.As soon as he touched me, my head lifted to meet him, snaking my tongue across his bottom lift until his came out, too.

I shoved against him. "Why do you keep doing that? I'm not a damn damsel in distress that you can just kiss to make things better."

Rylan looked almost offended. “I know you’re not a damsel. Do you think I’d have to do it if you were? Distraction is better than confrontation when this happens and it’s usually the first idea to pop up.”

“Of course it is.” I rolled my eyes but I understood. I wasn’t really mad, just annoyed at having to be taken care of and controlled.

I may have trouble controlling my powers and not want to stop but I hated the pop that went off in my head every time the fire took over. I didn't remember what happened very well when it found its way into my head.

I leaned my head back and Rylan took it as an invitation. I could feel my neck clearing up. There was something there. I didn’t worry about it, it wasn’t there now. I wrapped my arms around Rylan’s neck. He put his hands on my hips and pulled me towards him.

I could still feel my fangs. They didn’t go away. I bit down on Rylan’s lip. He made a small breathy noise. I didn’t break skin. I pulled away from him and I could feel my new teeth slide back into my gums.

Neither of us moved further, his hands still resting on my hips. “Thank you.”

I looked over his shoulder at Death. “Did it work?”

She shook her head. “Not as well as planned. But there is a collar that will keep you from harming anyone who doesn’t deserve it without my permission.”

“Like a freaking movie character.”

She tilted her head. “I do not believe I am familiar with this movie you speak of.”

“It’s part of a whole universe.”

Death just looked more and more confused. Rylan laughed, if maybe a little forced.

I smiled. “You gotta see it.”

Rylan stepped aside so we were side by side. “But the abridged version. The original version sucks.”

“She’s our only hope and you want to watch stupid show?” I don’t know which reaper it was that spoke but they were all looking at us. I faced them all.

Death went to speak but I put a hand up. “Honeys, if your only hope is me, then you better get used to the feeling of disappointment early.” I walked away, grabbing Rylan’s hand, who was still standing next to me, and Death’s hand, when I went to pass her.

I wish I knew what they were both thinking about all of this but I figured it out for myself. I love them both. I could accept that if they could. I knew eventually I would have to choose. I put it out of my head immediately. That time has not come up yet.

We walked towards the war room when my phone rang. I answered it without looking.

"Hello?" I didn't want to think that it was Death's hand I let go of to answer it.

"Rhydian? Please, it's, uh, time to come home."

"Mom?" I stopped in my tracks. "Mom, are you okay?"

"Honey, please." She sounded panicked. If I could picture her, I was sure she would be shaking and covered in sweat.

"What's going on, mom?" I heard her scream. "MOM!" I could hear a distinct laughter and I knew it wasn't from her.

"Where is she?"

I looked up at Rylan. "Illinois."

I turned to Death. "Send me to the bar where Allison found me." I needed to get to my bike. There's no way I could fly all the way over there.

"Go to her, D. Please. Find her. We have to make a few stops on the way if we're going to beat this son of a bitch."

Rylan looked at me. I nodded. "Got it," and he took off for his truck.

Death lifted my chin so I would look at her. I had been looking at him as he went. "Go now," and she tapped me on the forehead. My head was spinning.

I didn't even realize that I had closed my eyes against the sensation until I opened them again. The lighting was different. I blinked against it. Trying to get my eyes to adjust to the darkness. I was in the bar. I was back in Indiana. I don't even know how Allison found me in the first place. I didn't have time to think. I have to at least be able to save one of them. And mom's the only one left. I don't have a choice. I have to save her. He's playing mind games. And he's fucked with the wrong family.

I saw Jo at the bar and she started walking over.

"I didn't see you come in."

"I didn't."

I turned and walked out of the building. I knew where my bike was and I had to make this quick. There were two stops that I had to make so Rylan would probably beat me there, he only had to make one and he would end up closer than I will.

My bike was right where I left it. I didn't really think anybody would steal my baby. I would kill for this little beauty. I hopped on and revved her up. I reveled in the feel of her engine purring underneath me. I reveled in the human feel of it. No more wings. No more teleporting. Now I can drive. No need to run. Just to speed. I pulled out as quickly as my bike could take and sped off so fast the front tire wanted to come off the road. I leaned forward. Distribution. You get used to dealing with it when you have a small frame on a big bike. It didn't bother me anymore.

I had to stop by my hold hunting cabin. It was in Indiana, as well. That's actually why I was here in the first place. I was going to clear it out and send it all to Rylan. He was going to need it far more than I was. Especially since I had planned on killing myself the same night. That's why I was flirting with that girl. One more night of having a warm body next to me. I was going to send her away and hoped she would hear the shot so the cops would know where to find me. So that my mother no longer had to worry about me or my habits or my job.

The drive was going to be long, I already knew that but it was still daylight out so I had plenty of time. Just had to wonder. How much time did my mother have? Is she already dead? Why didn't I just let Death take me there?

I shook my head. No time to doubt myself now. There is no way of stopping Clark or whatever he has become without the stops I need to make. Just get the stuff and get to mom. Get the stuff and get to mom. No time for anything else.

The roads were surprisingly not busy so I drove far over the speed limit. I didn't think cop cars could even see me, since I passed three and none of them stopped me. I didn't care I wouldn't have stopped anyway. I have places to be and I will kill anyone I have to to get to them.

The cabin was only an hour from the bar I was at. The way I was driving, I could probably make it in thirty. I wasn't sure but I was guesstimating and I liked my odds. There were winding roads and fog and I didn't care about any of it. I could only see the cabin and my mother inside it, burning alive with fear and anger at what I was sure Clark was putting her through. I drove faster. I knew she wasn't in the cabin but it was one step closer to me getting her back.

Indiana is a reasonably wet state and driving erratically was dangerous but again I didn't care. Nothing was going to stop me. Until something did. Emphasis on something.

There was something in the middle of the road and I slid the bike so she was on her side, grinding against the road. My leg was pinned under her and I was just a hair away from hitting it. It growled.

"What the hell?"

I knew what it was. I could see three more around it, lingering a little bit further back. I did not have time for this. My hair lit up. Looks like these nice gentlemen aren't innocent. This was the one creature that did not want to mess with me. I could see two more in human form off towards the woods. On the road I needed to be on. It led to the cabin. How they even knew it was there I had no idea. Or maybe they didn't know at all. Maybe they were just following me. Yeah, that would have to be it. Anybody who knows about this cabin wouldn't tell someone who would tell a monster.

I could feel the flames getting bigger and broader and I was starting to smell gas. I looked down at the bike, the gas line was broken. My flames wouldn't hurt me but it would certainly burn their hairy asses. I focused on the gas line that was spewing all over me. It was shaking but soon it started to lift out of the hold it was in. It floated higher and higher.

I threw it at the one in front of me. It was my main concern. It soaked the mutt and it backed up, growling again.

"Come on, let's go." I threw a ball of flames at it. It sounded so cheesy and so middle school action flick but that is what I did and that was what I kept doing. The three that were still in their other forms ran over. One jumped over the bike so it missed the spewing gas. It bit down on my shoulder, enticing a scream from my throat. All that rage baking inside, letting it loose would be a great feeling. They were standing in my way. I wanted them dead. All of them.

I got choked back. I grabbed for my neck. The collar was back. What the hell? These were not innocents. I still had two more left. They walked over and one of them extended a hand. We were all very close and personal. They both inhaled, taking in my scent. I looked them in the eyes, both of them. One and then the other. They both did a slight nod of the head. And then they were gone. I was marked for later but at least they were out of my way for now. It was definitely the weirdest encounter I've ever had with werewolves. I killed their own and they let me go.

I was glad they did. I don't know how much of my power I can use before this collar takes it away. I don't know how much I can use while it is on. I can fight but werewolves have teeth. I smiled. I guess I do now, too.

I ruffled my feathers and stretched out my wings. I guess I was flying from here. I bent at the knees and leapt upwards. My wings caught me on a downward stroke and up I was. This would probably be faster but I wasn't sure how much I could carry. I would have preferred my bike.

I followed the side road and I could see the cabin. And I was in dismay. It was burning to the ground. That's why they were here before me. Waiting for me. They wanted to make sure I didn't get what I came for. Good thing I wasn't stupid enough to leave it in the house.

I inhaled slightly. The fire wavered towards me. I landed on the edge of the wood around it and walked the rest of the way up. I focused with my hands extended towards the flames. I've only done this once before. How hard could it be to do it again? I inhaled again. And I tried to take it all in. I pulled and pulled like it was a tug-of-war that would result in life or death and I had to win it. I threw my hands up and it looked like there were fireworks in the air tonight. I just needed somewhere to throw the spare flames. I didn't want to bring it inside. It wasn't mine. And it wasn't like back on the compound, that was dire. This was just a nuisance.

I walked over to the burnt remains of a shell I used to call home. This cabin had been passed down in my mother's family for the longest time. It was, after all, my mother who was a hunter first. Not my dad, who was the one who stuck the landing with it all. Mom just quit. I guess I have more of her in me than I thought. And so many memories, just gone.

I ignored the house for the rest of my short visit. There was nothing more that I could do for it. No need to get teary eyed. Spilt milk and all that. I walked over to the well that was on the other side of the house. Most hunters would have just thrown a waterproof bag into it but I didn't have time for all that. I hit the side of the little wooden roof and a bag came tumbling out. I almost didn't catch it and it would've dropped down into the water. The bag wasn't even waterproof. Stupid, on my part. But I caught it.

I didn't have to check to make sure everything was there. The weight was all the same and the seal of the bag hasn't been tampered with. I was ready to go. I opened it up and grabbed some throwing knives. I strapped a gun to my thigh and placed one in a holder in my waistline. I also grabbed a contractible katana blade and set it in a shealth on my back. And I looked at the leather jacket that was in the bottom of the bag. It was my mom's. I left it in there for her. I could still smell her on it, even within the thick carcass of the bag. I put it to my nose and took a big whiff. I haven't seen mom since Allison's funeral. I'll have to tell her what happened to her daughter, again. Tears threatened to spill over onto my face. I shook them away. Now is not the time, I told myself.

It was time to go. I could hear howls in the distance. Maybe the little fur babies decided they were hungry. Well, unless they could fly, they were not my problem and they were shit out of luck. I put the straps over my shoulders and clipped the two bands over my chest and around my waist. It wasn't going anywhere but I was, I launched myself back into the sky.

9 WITH NEW EYES

Flying put a whole new perspective on things. It would be nice to think I could just come out here and fly over the wooded area or over the town only miles away. I could see the lights. Little twinkling stars in the distance. It truly was amazing. But I didn't have time to focus on that. I had to focus on making it to my next location. It's been awhile since the last time I've been there. And I really should've made time to go back sooner. Dad would be pissed if he knew I didn't visit him. He probably does know. Maybe that's why I have such bad luck.

I doubt it was my father's fault that everyone around me was dying and I had all sorts of monsters from Hell chasing me. Literally. I just made stupid decisions. And now they were all starting to catch up with me. Everyone around me were the ones who were paying the price for me.

I wondered what he would say about all of this. Hell opening up. Me being in a relationship with Death. I think he would like

Rylan better, not by much, though. He probably would have killed Allison a second time. He didn't deal with monsters well. He definitely would have killed me by now. It wouldn't even phase him that I was his daughter. And that was an interesting thing to be aware of as a monster, as a daughter, as a hunter. It's partially why he split with mom. It was always so black and white with him while mom couldn't take it anymore. She was never a cruel woman, even if it was better if she was. She left before she had to watch him kill his own daughters. I think she knew what I would become and couldn't handle it herself. I wasn't the reason she left, not really at least. I knew that. But I couldn't help but believe that I was a little part of it all.

I wondered what she would think of the woman I have become. Of the monster I've become. She would accept me, she wouldn't like it but she would welcome me in with open arms. The only reason we chose not to talk was because I chose dad. I chose not to leave the life with her. It was all I've ever known. Little did it matter that once he died and my sister died, I did leave. I never told her that I quit. I let her believe I was out every night doing God knows what to make this shitty little world a better, somewhat safer place. I couldn't bring myself to face her again.

Knowing that I got my father killed by not going with him. By getting my baby sister killed by not listening to her when she told me she wasn't ready. God, why didn't I ignore my father's orders and listen to my sister for once? If I wasn't so hard headed, they could both still be here.

The tears that were coming from my eyes had no effect on me. The wind from the speed I was taking stole them right away. Like they never happened. It reminded me of how Clark easily threw my sister away. Like their love never happened. I tried to imagine doing that to Rylan or to Death. I couldn't even fathom the disease that must be cursing his brain to make him do such a thing and not have it affect him in any way whatsoever. Maybe he was crazy. It wouldn't stop me from killing him though. Nothing would.

I kept on flying. I had to get through a whole state. Nothing was going to stop me from getting to my mother. I kept telling that to myself over and over again. Nothing. Nothing. Nothing. I could not lose another family member. Death should already be there and I felt that she could find a way to let me know if something had happened to her. Rylan should be close by. His stop should have been short. Unless the witch was still lurking there, or he had company waiting for him like I did. At least I could have sworn we killed that witch. After all she did kill *his* mother.

I thought through my entire life. It had only one consistency. Death. It had been following me around all my life. Maybe that was why Death was so fond of me. She has known me for years. I was surprised that I haven't cracked from being around it constantly. I was surprised I haven't figured it out before. I was surprised that I haven't seen all of this coming. Killing so many things and so many people was bound to bring bad luck. And here it was. Sitting on my doorstep like a stray dog that I made the mistake of feeding once. It just keeps coming back for more and more. And you let it. I let Death in. I let her in and she made herself nice and cozy. That was before we officially met. For some reason it didn't bother me as much as it probably should have. Once we did meet, I was instantly drawn to her. Kind of like an old friend. I could tell she felt it, too. I knew it should have bothered me. Her being a part of all the death that followed my family around. But it didn't. She was just doing her job. I wondered if she ever got tired of it. I know I already have and I just have to deal with my family, not the whole world.

Dad's burial site was in a normal cemetery and it just happened to be in Illinois. I would only be hours away from my mother which I could probably fly in about 20 minutes, if I had to guess. Hopefully that wouldn't be twenty minutes too late. I could see the cemetery a few seconds later. It had begun to rain and my wings were feeling heavy. I don't know if it was from the extra weight being added or because of the cargo I was hauling. I had to land soon. I made it to the edge of the graves when I made a stumbling landing. I fell to my knees. More like skidded.

I sat there in the mud for a second. I felt like I had to say some words of peace or something over his grave. But I was never much for words. Neither was he, maybe he wouldn't mind. When I got up, I didn't even have to think about where he was resting. I've lurked in this cemetery so many times. I rarely made it over to his tombstone. But I would sit and watch for a while. He didn't need my protection but I missed my chance in life so I might as well watch over him in death. I'd always look out for my loved ones too late. It was the curse that I bore.

I made my way over. I weaved through tombstones, some new and some old. I thought about all the families attached to these stones. I wondered if any of them died a horrible death. Maybe they would have something to talk about with my father. I hoped he wasn't lonely.

And there it was. Mark Gregerson. Loving father. Caring husband. That's all it said. It said nothing about how he lived. Or how he died. But I understood. We can't just put his business in the public eye in a goddamn rock. And the public eye does not want to know our business. There would be hysteria.

I sat in front of his headstone and rested my head against it. It was cold to the touch. The exact opposite of how I felt inside. I reached my hand down and pulled out the flowers that were planted there. When the roots were exposed, there was a small piece of ribbon attached to it. I pulled it and the headstone moved. Only slightly. It exposed a small but deep hole and I reached down and pulled out three guns, three ammo boxes, and six grenades. All of which were my father's, I thought it best to keep them with him.

I lifted my head up from the stone. My ears perked and I jerked my head to the side.

Do you ever get that feeling that you're being watched? It might just be me with my heightened senses always on alert. I stood up and looked around me.

"Hello?" I stepped away from my father's stone. Like an axe murderer would say something backed. I looked into a small patch of woods. Very small. There was about five trees in one small spot. Perfect hiding place. I saw the leaves rustle. Of course it could have been the wind but I doubt it with my luck.

A gun was already in my hand. "Hey, I know you're there!" I walked towards the trees but I stopped in my tracks immediately. Because a figure came out of the little patch of woods. I put a hand over my mouth. The figure was wearing dirty combat boots, the real ones because he was actually in the military. The torn jeans were so familiar to me that a little gasp escaped me. I closed my eyes against the worn, warm flannel that cloaked his broad shoulders. The five o'clock shadow that always rested on his ruggedly handsome face that has seen far too much. And the black hair that never grew longer than a buzz cut.

"Daddy?"

"Aren't you a little old to be calling me that?"

I stood up straighter, my eyes instantly vacant of tears. "Yes, sir." I stood there, trying to figure out what to say.

"You're not supposed to be here. You need to move on."

He shook his head, like he was about to dumb something down for me. "You can't do this without me. Look at what you're becoming. We hunted the things that you are headed towards."

"I'm not evil, dad." I walked forward and I kept walking, I went through him," I have to go. Mom needs my help."

"Yeah, I figured that's what you were gathering my supplies for. But it won't matter. You can't save her."

I stopped. I was tired of letting him walk all over me. Telling me what I can and cannot do. I let him do it my entire life, I would be damned if I let him do it when he wasn't even alive.

"Why? Because I couldn't save you? You wouldn't let me go with you. It took me three days to find all the pieces that were left of you 'cause you wanted to go off half cocked. So why? Because I couldn't save Allison. I did the same thing to her that you did to me. The only difference is that I survived. So my bad that I wanted to be like you. Tell me why."

I sucked in a breath and continued, "Because I couldn't save myself? Because that is your fault! You were the one who brought me to the witch's hut. You were the one fighting the wrong goddamn monster. I am so sorry that I am becoming a monster. But I am going to do whatever it takes to save the last of my loved ones. So get the hell out of my face or tell me why goddamn it!"

I was screaming by the end of it but I didn't care. Nobody was there to stop me. Nobody was going to hear me. And I can't exactly wake the dead.

I watched him shake his head and I bit my lip to keep from screaming. He looked over his shoulder and another figure appeared.

"That's not what I meant."

"No."

"That's why you cannot save me, darling. I'm already dead."

"No, mom." I stumbled back and tried to touch her head but I went through her. I feathered my fingers around her face. "You were the last one."

She placed a hand gently against my face, not quite touching but as close as she could come to it. “No. *You* are the last one.”

“Did Death even make it to you?”

“No, I did not.”

I felt Death behind me. I didn’t look. “Why didn’t you tell me?”

“You needed to see it for yourself. You needed to talk to them.” I felt Death place a hand on my shoulder. My eyes had begun to burn.

“Hey, control yourself.” My dad barked. I took a step back, moving closer into Death.

“That is enough.” I saw Death reach a hand out and wave a finger. Dad disappeared.

I looked around, panicked. “Where did he go?”

“Where he belonged. He’s home now.”

Mom leaned forward and kissed me on the cheek though I couldn’t feel it. “I’m ready, as well.”

Death walked around me and I saw her nod. Another wave of her finger and my mother was gone, too.

I took a deep breath. I felt... Free. I had no idea that my father was lingering over me for so long. Haunting me. Now he was gone. I can feel the weight being lifted off my shoulders. Which is so cliche but that’s exactly how I felt. The weight I felt when it started to rain. It wasn't the water at all. I felt my mother die and I didn't even know.

I sighed. "Death?"

"Yes, my dear."

"When did we first meet?"

Death gave a little chuckle but it didn't sound happy. "The night you were born. There was an infant that had died in the crib next to yours, awaiting his parents. You wouldn't stop crying. All I did was pull your blanket over you and you looked at me with a wisdom I found remarkable."

"Guess I was a special baby to catch your attention."

"You certainly were, my dear."

"Did you keep tabs on me?"

"Every once in a while, I would make sure you were alright, yes, but I never interfered, since that is what you seem to be inquiring."

I rubbed a hand over my face. I turned to look at Death. "Come on, I want to see her body." I walked past her back to where I dropped my bag.

Or I tried to. Death put an arm across my chest and grabbed my shoulder. "You have one more visitor." I shook my head, eyes wide. I don't think I can handle seeing my baby sister.

"Hello, Rhyder." I closed my eyes and just opened my arms. I could feel a slight tingle across my entire front. It was the closest thing to a hug that we could get. I opened my eyes and looked up. I blew out hot air.

"Hey, Ally." My voice was a hoarse replica of what it should've sounded like. I grazed where her head would be, pretending I was actually petting her hair like I used to.

She pushed back slightly, which means she drifted through my arms. I let my arms fall to my side. "I love you." Death didn't wave a finger or make a noise. She just started to drift away. She was fading into nonexistence.

I waited until she was completely gone. "I love you, too."

"Time to go?" I looked up at Death, I'm sure looking just as innocent and scared as I felt.

She nodded. "Yes, love. It is time to go." Death moved one arm out from behind her. The movement produced a big cargo bag. She was holding my bag. I smiled but it was small and very forced. She held her arms open for me. I walked into them. I was far too tired to fly and I would bet that I was about to be exhausted.

I was right. I sat down on the couch in my mother's adorable little house. My head was in my hands. She was lying in the kitchen. This was the first time that I have ever been to her house, the first time being inside. That sounds creepy but I just wanted her safe. And now she was dead. And it was my fault. Rylan was sitting next to me, rubbing my back.

Death was with her. I think she was doing some juju magic. She explained it to me. She's going to make sure that my mother's body is buried next to my father's since we don't have a family plot. Mom did pick the location for him so that in the future they could be buried together. It didn't matter that they were divorced, she wanted to be with him. If I was a betting girl, I would say they are together right now. I don't know if that's how heaven or hell or wherever they are works. But if anyone could find a way to be together then I bet it would be them.

"I have to get out of here. I have to find him. I'm going back to the compound." I said it so abruptly that Rylan jumped and Death looked over. Of course Death would have known what I was about to say.

"I am finished here. Let us go home." We all stood and headed for the door. Death put a hand on both of our shoulders.

"Time to go." We looked at each other and we were gone. I caught a scent right before we vanished. I started hitting against Death, trying to get her to let go of me.

"How could you?" When I could talk again, I opened my eyes and we were at the compound. Right in front of the ladder to the houses. She let me go.

Rylan looked confused. "What?"

"He was there, I could smell him," I looked back towards Death, I shoved her, "Why didn't you let me kill him?"

"It would destroy you."

"I don't care! I need to destroy him!" I shoved her again. And she let me. We both knew she could stop me.

"Rhyd, calm down."

"I am calm! Stay out of this, Rylan." Flames started to appear in my hair. I could feel them floating around. Floating across my body. Like I was water and it was dye. I did need to calm down, I didn't want to hurt her, not really.

"Get out of my face. I can't stand to look at you right now." And just like that, she was gone. I don't know where she went and I didn't really care at the moment. Later, I knew, I would feel bad but as of right now, I let the hurt in her eyes fuel me. I climbed the rope up to the cabin that I had been sharing with Death.

I flopped on the bed. Rylan sat on the edge and for some reason I didn't want him there. But I really wanted him here. I crawled forward and ran my hands up his back and over his shoulders. I kissed the back of his neck and licked the little sensitive spot behind his ear, just the way I knew he liked.

I let the anger fuel me and it quickly turned into something else. "Is it time to play?" I whispered in his ear. He looked back at me. I nibbled on the edge of his ear and rubbed myself against his back. I could hear his breath hitch.

"Yeah, baby, it's time to play." Rylan turned around to me and glanced over his shoulder. Then he moved a lot faster than I expected and flipped me over so I was on my back. I bit my lip and laughed. I let my legs fall apart so he would have room to lean down to me. I opened my mouth in a gasp but he didn't kiss me like I wanted him to. I pouted.

Rylan chuckled. He ran his hands up my body until he extended my arms above my head and pinned me there. He brought his knees forward, forcing my legs further apart, causing a small noise to escape me. I tried to pull my arms from his grasp so I could touch him but the way I was pinned made it difficult.

He kissed down my neck and I rolled us over. "*I* want to play."

"Go ahead, baby. I'm not going to stop you." I laughed again. I laid against him slowly and kissed him.

Slowly, I trailed a line of kisses down his chin to his throat. My tongue snaked out and licked him, I immediately grazed my teeth against that same spot and reveled in the moan that escaped his lips. My hips grinded against his and his fingers dug into my skin as he held me tighter. I returned to his lips and kissed him deeply.

I felt a snap in my head, I tried to fight it but it never worked before, I shouldn't have expected it to work now. I shot up. I didn't get off of him but I stopped kissing him. I tried to move so I was no longer sitting on him. Rylan grabbed my hips and held me in place.

"I'm so sorry." I tried to get off of him once again but he held me still.

"Don't be, baby, it's alright."

He sat up with me still on his lap and put his hands on each side of my head and kissed me. Giving me plenty of time to pull away. I let him. Soon enough, the fire was back. He started to kiss down my chest even though we both had all of our clothes still on. I grabbed his head and pulled him close. My head fell back and I wanted to be rough with him. I wanted him to be rough with me. But suddenly, I growled and looked up. I continued to hold him against me. Mine. I looked around and growled again. Something wasn't right. I stood up on my knees insteading of laying on top of him on the bed and rocked above Rylan.

"Oh, baby, keep doing that."

I looked down, he had closed his eyes and I realized what I was doing. I stopped shifting but I didn't move. I hadn't spotted the danger yet.

Do you ever feel an obnoxious urge to get up and do something? I was feeling that. I was feeling that at the wrong moment. I got off of Rylan and looked out the window. I looked around the room again. I crawled back over to the bed and slithered my way back on top of Rylan.

"Stay here." With each word, I tapped his lips. I crawled back off and stood in front of him.

Something was telling me that I needed to be outside. I went to the door and looked out. I closed my eyes. I felt very light, swaying back and forth. I put a hand on one side of the door frame and let my body weight spin me outside. My head lulled to one side. Rylan caught my arm. I shrugged him off.

"Hey."

"Something's wrong." I went outside. I looked out over the entire compound. I grabbed a hold of the railing and flipped myself over. I twisted in the middle like an actual gymnast and looked out again. I hung there for a while. When I let go, I landed right in front of the ladder. It hit me from the wind and I caught myself on fire. I don't take being startled well.

I followed the feeling and it led me down to the fighting pit. I thought the feeling reminded me of Death. Maybe she needed to show me something. I sucked in a breath and smiled. Maybe she went and led him here. It doesn't really matter. She wanted me to know he was here and I was insanely enraptured. I liked to have fun. And my collar's off when he's around. How exciting. I actually jumped up and down like a small child. I made a small twirl and landed in the middle of the fighting pit.

"He's here. I can smell him." I searched the area around me.

"What?" I heard Rylan's voice but I didn't focus on that. He was still trying to catch up to me.

I don't know what called me out of the house but something did and I thanked god for it. I was not going to miss my chance. Not again.

"Where's Death? We could use her help." Rylan had followed me out of the little house we were in. It was Death's cabin but I was starting to think about it differently. And for once I was glad Death wasn't there to hear it.

"I don't care. He's mine."

I looked back at him. "Now it's time to really play."

"I don't understand."

"He's here, I don't know why I knew to come out here but I did. Now I can smell him. He wants me to know he's here."

"What do we do?"

"Catch him. This is not our first hunt." God, he was really starting to ruin my buzz. I pouted again.

He hesitated. “Maybe we should try to find D...”

“Rylan, it’s now or never, I have to find him. So either sit there and shut up and wait for my signal or go back inside. What’s it going to be?”

He sighed. “Goddamn it, Rhyd. You know what I’m gonna say.”

“Good,” I stopped looking around, “Then we have work to do.”

I made a circle in the dirt around me. I don’t really know why but it felt right. I heard something flying towards us, it hooed. It sounded small and familiar.

“Martin!”

“Hello, young warrior. I am here to deliver something to you.” That’s when I noticed a small bottle in one of his talons.

“Death had been saving this for a very long time and thought now would be the time to bring it back into the light.”

“What is it?” I took it from him and looked at it. It was a greenish liquid. It looked disgusting.

“If I reveal the contents to you then I am afraid you would not drink it.”

I laughed, he had a good point. I held it up. “What’s it for?”

"Ah, that question I have an answer for. It is for healing. Take it before you get injured and you will be able to heal yourself."

I looked back at Rylan then the bottle again, once again landing on Martin. I already knew what I was going to do with it.

"But I can already heal myself."

"I am doing as I am told. It is yours to do with what you wish."

I instantly tossed it over to Rylan. "You'll need it more than me."

He almost tossed it back. "She gave it to you."

"And I'm giving it to you. Drink up." He knew it was a useless argument. He downed it in one go. Thank god for all those trips and investigations in bars. I had to speak rather loudly because out of nowhere winds were pushing against us. The Dark Cloud or whatever Death called it. Looks like more are finally coming. It's almost here. We won't be waking up in the same world in the morning. If we're still alive by then.

10 ALL HAIL

I knelt down on the grund and closed my eyes. I felt the compound's floor. If any vibration was going to come through, I would feel it. I tilted my head. Someone was coming from the other side. The outskirts of the compound. He wanted to make sure I knew he was here. I stood up and listened more intently. He was off towards my right. Rylan waited until I gave him the signal. I waited until he was closer.

"On the right! Twenty yards! Go!" I took off. Rylan did, as well.

We all ran into the woods. It was like a bad movie. Clark hit the woods and disappeared. Shortly after, I followed behind. Lastly, Rylan crept in behind me. I was glad that I never left the compound and gave up. I never would have been able to learn the ins and outs of these woods. I could hear Rylan stumbling somewhere behind me. I didn't stop to look. I just kept going. I had to keep going.

I jumped over fallen branches and twisted around trees. I came up on a small dirt mound but I took it too fast and ended up in the air. I let it flow through me and caught a branch. I'm sure the sight was very amusing. A girl very angrily swinging from tree limb to tree limb. I thought it slowed me down but I ended up right above Clark.

Letting go of a branch, I hoped to drop right on top of him. It didn't work out that way. He managed to pick up the pace and ran past me. I landed on my feet and my hands to catch me from toppling over. I looked up, my hair falling out in front of my face. I gave chase once again.

He was a lot faster than I remembered. I never focused on his speed when we were fighting. Hand to hand, I was the faster of the two. Long distance, it looked like he was. I tried to push it. I tried to put all my anger and hatred to fuel my legs and my lungs. It didn't look like I was going to catch him. I wouldn't let him get away. I can't let him get away.

"He's going to get away!" That was Rylan from behind me. Echoing my very thoughts.

"Like hell he is." I put everything I had into running faster and harder, trying to get to him. I groaned at the amount of work I was forcing my body to do. But I only had to be faster for a few more seconds. I was only inches away. I could see my fingers stretching out to grab his shirt. I pushed my wings down and gave a hard flap outward, forcing myself to lunge forward.

I tackled him, grabbing a hold of his legs. We rolled and separated. I landed on one knee and I saw Clark start to crawl away. He got up and faced me. With a gun in his hand. I didn't even notice that he had one on him. I figured if he had one he would've shot us a long time ago. Save us all the effort of the chase.

"Where are you going, huh? This place lands on a cliff, you know that. So what? You gonna kill me like you killed my sister, Clark?"

Rylan came up beside me, pointing his gun right back at Clark, he didn't seem to mind. He kept his weapon aimed directly on me, never wavering. He never lost his focus on me. That's when Clark threw his gun down and started to laugh. Rylan didn't ease up on his.

"You think that idiot could have done what I've done? You think he had the balls? I should be insulted!" Clark who apparently wasn't Clark had to yell over the roar of the wind.

"Come on, Clark, there's nowhere for you to go, why'd you do it?" This came from

Rylan, who was now standing slightly in front of me.

He laughed. "You idiots truly don't get it, do you? Here let me spell it out for you. I. Am. Not. Clark. Although I had you all fooled. The name's Michael." He actually looked cocky.

"What'd Death ever do to you?" I rushed before he had a chance to distract us with whatever story he was about to spin. I didn't particularly care about the why or the explanation. I cared about the who and I knew that already.

"Death?" Clark/Michael laughed, "You think this has to do with Death? No, sweet cheeks, this is all about you." I racked my brain for anything that could tell me what the hell he was talking about. I looked over my shoulder. The storm was coming faster and it would be here soon.

"What's she got to do with this?" Rylan took a step forward, in front of me. Always the protector.

I stepped closer, too. It was hard to hear over the wind and we didn't have much time left. I kept thinking about everything I knew about Clark. Then it hit me. I thought he was oddly familiar to me when we first met but

I couldn't put my finger on what it was back then. I think I remembered it now.

"June 3rd, 2012. I was sixteen years old. Michael was twenty-three at the time. He just had a mental break and that was when Clark was created, right?" Rylan just looked at me. It was all falling into place now.

Once I started, I couldn't stop, I remembered every little thing about that night. After all, it was my first human kill. "Dad, Allison, and I were on a hunt. We'd been tracking a pack of werewolves for the past three months when we caught a whiff of something down in Chicago. We thought we'd bite, we weren't getting anywhere with the mutts." I stepped forward again when I noticed Michael stepped back, I stopped, he was backing himself into a cliff and I wasn't even sure if he knew it but I wasn't done with him yet.

"Something was killing people violently. But no hunter could figure it out. We thought maybe some vampires or some rogue ghouls but nothing would stick. It ended up being a Carnivora, like a hybrid between the two. Most hunters have never even heard of them, that was my first experience with one. It turns out that thing wasn't the only one killing. Michael was, too. It was almost unheard of. Someone with multiple personalities usually has the timid, nice version of themselves up front and originally. This wasn't the case with you. You were a murderous bastard beforehand. But I didn't know he was killing until I stumbled upon a crime in progress, assuming that he was the Carnivora, I tried to stop him. Later, I found out he was only human. That you were only human."

"You killed him." Rylan said, with understanding. I nodded.

"Killed me? She didn't just kill me. She tore me apart while I was still alive. Are you familiar with the ways to kill a Carnivora? Cause I wasn't until then!"

Rylan looked at me. I swallowed the rock that was in my throat. "You have to cut off all the limbs but they have to be alive while you do it so they don't just come back and grow new limbs. You have to kill their spirit in the process by cutting out their hearts."

"All while they were still alive? It would've seemed like torture to someone who didn't know any better." Rylan was trying to defend me. "She didn't know any better. She killed you."

"You're damn right she did it! She didn't even blink twice before she threw those daggers into my chest, and taking me apart, piece by piece. I was human!"

"You were a killer!" My reckless decision tore me apart for weeks until I got it through my thick head that I saved so many people by getting rid of one.

"So you got to know my sister once you realized who she was, pretended to love her, started killing reapers because you knew she would come to me, then you killed her. For what? For revenge? All so you could kill me?" I was screaming, partly because of the wind but mostly because of the rage that was welling up inside me. I could feel my eyes beginning to burn.

"I didn't want to kill you. Oh, no, that would be too simple. No, I wanted you to pay. You took my life in the most painfully gruesome way you could probably think of and it would just be way too easy to take your life. So I took everybody else's."

He laughed again and I threw one of my daggers into his leg. I didn't want to kill him, either. I wanted to take my time. The storm was already in the woods and closing in. Time I didn't have.

I walked toward him when he began to scream but Death was right behind him before

I could make it to him. I started to run. “NO!” But she hovered over the cliff with him.

I'm doing this to save you.

I wanted to destroy him and she was going to take that away from me.

I have found that I can love, my dear, and I love you. I am terribly sorry that I have to go. That's when I realized what she was doing. I ran faster, “No, wait! Don't!”

She whispered in Michael's ear, “I am sorry, my child.” She tapped his forehead and I could just see his whole face change. Clark was back and he looked very confused. Then all at once he seemed at peace.

Death whispered it again, “I am so sorry, my child.” That's when Clark smiled. I had wondered if he was there when Michael was doing the killing. I think he was. Just not when he was Clark again. And what he said next confirmed it for me.

He smiled, “Thank you.” Death looked at me, she had her palms out, and she blew something towards me. A white cloud of smoke encircled me. And she fell from the sky and with Clark in her arms. I don't know what it was that she blew but I could feel it affecting me immediately. I fell to my knees.

Rylan ran over and tried to pick me up. I coughed. My eyes were still burning. I had just gotten to my feet when we both looked up. We were out of time. We didn't have any place to go and no time to get there. I pushed Rylan to the ground and squatted over him. In my head, I pictured that I was holding a ball, just a little small sphere. I envisioned myself tracing the ball with my hands, all the way around, and around and around. I saw it getting bigger and bigger.

"Jesus!" I could barely hear Rylan but I heard the awe in the panic of his voice. I knitted my eyebrows together, trying to focus harder. The blue ball in my hands was growing. By the end, we were completely surrounded by my blue ball of fire. I opened my eyes, not entirely realizing I closed them, the ball was real.

I was shaking from the force of the storm. Death called it a Dark Cloud. Not an apocalypse but it'll be bad. Hell spawns from all over will be escaping from their little holes to come out and play. I kept telling myself it'll all be over soon. Because if I didn't, I would drop the shield and we would surely both be dead.

I was pushed to the ground by the strength of the wind. Or it could have been something else. I couldn't be too sure with my eyes closed against the strain. I was already on my knees, being pushed lower and lower, I was bending as low as I could go without suffocating Rylan. It was getting harder and harder to breathe, as if I was still stuck in the strong breeze. Trying to make my sphere as small and as tight as possible. I wouldn't be able to last much longer.

"That's it. Enough!" I struggled to stand, my knees buckled multiple times at each burst. I looked at everything around me and just stopped. I stopped imagining that protective barrier around us. I stopped focusing. And I could breathe again.

I pushed all of that energy and tension out. And I could see it. It was like a wave moving towards the storm. I could see the clouds being pushed back. Nothing came near us. Everything dissolved, completely disappeared and I could see the sky again. It was night. I had lost track of time, I wasn't really sure anymore. What I was sure of was a white cloud of smoke went up into the sky. I took a step towards it and I noticed that it was in the vague shape of a skull and crossbones.

That's when an excruciating pain came over me. I fell on my back, crushing my wings.

I tried to scream. Nothing came out. I arched my back to try and get away from it. My eyes burned. Turning into their flames to try and protect themselves. But from what? Myself?

I rolled over to my stomach and curled up. Rylan had me pinned to the ground so I wouldn't move anymore. So I wouldn't jump up and slaughter a whole town in a haze. I could feel the ends of my hair being pulled. Felt like someone was yanking them all out at once.

"Woah," I heard Rylan gasped. He leaned in as to not startle me and whispered, "Your hair is changing colors. It's… it's black." That's when the pain turned into more of a chill. It took over my whole body.

I looked at him. I had a feeling the fire in my eyes would stay like that forever. And oddly enough, I came to terms with that.

"What'd she do to you?"

I smiled up at him, and put a hand on his cheek. I lowered it until I could feel the pulse in his neck and I squeezed it. He wasn't expecting that and his eyes began to get wide and bulge away from his skull. I could feel his pulse quicken. Trying to fight against my hold. To fight to stay alive. It wouldn't work.

"Rhyd, don't. Please stop." It was barely a mumble but I heard it as if it was a scream. I kept my hold. I brought him very close to me and blew something into his open mouth. I wasn't exactly sure what to do but I knew what *it* would do.

Rylan's pulse slowed and then it stopped altogether. I set him down gently. It took minutes longer than I thought it would. I sat curled up against a tree near him. I just killed him, I kept whispering to myself. The guilt was going to eat me alive. I held my head in my hands, grabbing at my hair. If I felt pain, I could wait just a little bit longer. That's when he stirred. I crawled over to him as quickly as I could. I was the first thing he saw when he opened his eyes.

"Welcome back, Rylan." I smiled and helped him up.

I started to walk away. "What'd you do to me?"

I stopped and looked over my shoulder at him. 'You're gonna live forever." He crept closer to me.

"I'm a reaper now, aren't I?"

I nodded and turned, continuing on my trek back to the compound. "How'd you do that?"

I beckoned him to come with me. He did. "Rhyd?"

I laughed. The fire in my eyes burned even brighter. The heat overwhelmed me and mixed well with the new chill of my body.

"Please," I purred, "Call me Death."

www.ingramcontent.com/pod-product-compliance
Lightning Source LLC
LaVergne TN
LVHW091312150826
845673LV00006B/1616

9798678810809